Juan Sa

The
Unreported
Crime

Robert C. Stewart

Juan Santos in
The Unreported Crime

TO

Mother, PAT, Connie, Claire & Robert

Robert C. Stewart

CHAPTER ONE

"*This is the city, West Palm Beach, Florida. The boss is my dad, George. I have no partner. My name is Santos. I carry a mop. I was working the night watch...*"

"Hey kid, get back to work!" Juan was daydreaming, leaning on his mop, when another janitor spotted him. He waved at the other man and started working again. He was mopping the restrooms on the second floor of the 4th Street Police Station.

He told himself, "*The faster I work, the more time I'll have to sit in the squad room on my break.*" Juan hated his job and he kept telling himself that it was only temporary, but that didn't help much.

Juan was 17 years old and 170 pounds. He was of better than average height with a slim build, short cropped brown hair and serious brown eyes. Juan had graduated from high school just last month. He had hoped he would be able to relax for a couple of weeks and then join the Marines. No such luck. "*Thanks a lot, Rose! My dumb sister had to go and get married. Now I have to work and help pay for her stupid wedding. It's like the family traded her future for mine. Now it's going to take three years for the family to get out of debt.*"

Juan had been mumbling to himself about his predicament every day since his father was able to get him the job on his janitorial crew. The job with Acme Janitorial Services paid better than any kid fresh out high school could hope to expect. The downside, besides the manual labor, was that 90 percent of Juan's salary was turned over to his dad to help with the family finances. Juan was doing his best to look on the bright side. He always wanted to be a cop and now he was working in a police station.

Juan tried to take advantage of his situation. When he was at work, Juan spent every minute he could spare in the detectives' squad room looking at the cases in progress. He also signed up to take classes at the community college. Juan's new plan was to complete the course work required to take the Florida Department of Law Enforcement State Certification Examination. The course work was designed to be completed in six months, working full time. Juan was sure he could complete it in three years part-time.

He would never admit it to his father that he liked anything about the work, but Juan was happy being able to have complete access to the Investigative Services area of the station. Here on the night shift, he couldn't see the detectives at work, but he could follow their progress on major cases by looking at the reports they carelessly left on their desks and by observing the office whiteboards and corkboards containing pictures of suspects and case facts. Even the trash cans contained interesting items if you knew what you were looking for.

Unfortunately, technology was alive and well in the squad room and each detective had a password-protected computer. And most of the latest and juiciest information was locked away in those little boxes. Juan knew that moving papers around on somebody's desk was one thing, but accessing someone's computer was crossing the line. On the plus side, from Juan's point of view, anytime officers wanted to share information with each other, they printed it out. It seemed like everything got printed, judging from the amount of paper that had to be hauled away every day.

Juan started cleaning the interrogation rooms and empty holding areas; he saved the detectives' squad room for last. He even took his breaks there if no one was around. Between pouring over newspaper crime reporting and observing the surroundings in the squad room, Juan had a good idea of what was going on with all the high profile crimes in the city. He was interested in everything that was happening, but he always chose one crime to follow in detail.

The high priority crime of the moment was a murder case. The wife of a prominent doctor was found dead in her home, shot twice. The wife was having an affair and had sex shortly before her death. The doctor had been out of town for three days when the murder occurred. There was no forced entry. According to the detectives' notes, the doctor didn't appear to be broken up about the murder.

The police were going after the boyfriend hard. He had no alibi. They had gotten a warrant and searched the boyfriend's apartment, and found letters sent between the lovers, and keys to the victim's home. They confiscated the boyfriend's computer, but found nothing incriminating. According to the letters and e-mails, the two genuinely cared for each other.

Anyone with access to the detective offices could have obtained all the case information just by looking at the walls and the desktops. The whiteboard in the conference room had the case's timeline and several theories of the crime. Juan was sure that he could add or modify a theory and no one would notice.

He had his own theory. Juan suspected the doctor was working with someone to get rid of his wife. In Juan's version, the doctor had a mistress who shot the wife after the boyfriend's visit. The doctor could have given the mistress the key, which she used and got rid of. Juan thought his theory was just as good as any of the others. He didn't think the detectives in the department were very good anyway.

Juan was taking his break in the conference room. Looking at the whiteboard, he thought, *"Why not?"* He put on his rubber gloves, picked up a marker and with his left hand he wrote:

Doctor affair?

He thought, *"What harm can it do?"*

CHAPTER TWO

Just past 1:00 am, while Juan was working at the station, two young men were entering the liquor store on Congress Avenue across from the Tony's Pizza strip mall. They stepped in the door and split up and walked to opposite sides of the store. They moved slowly around the perimeter, taking note of the security camera's placement. The taller one, Eddie, had black hair, a thin mustache and permanent five o'clock shadow, which made him look as sinister as he actually was. He picked up a 24-ounce bottle of Coke and walked to the cashier. The other young man, Joey, had brown hair, a medium build and he moved around the store clumsily. He walked past the checkout counter and left the store. Eddie paid for the Coke and joined Joey outside.

"It's perfect," said Eddie. "One stationary security camera, one clerk and the freeway is two minutes away. We could be in, out and on the other side of town in ten minutes."

Joey was being his usual negative self. "I don't know. Maybe the clerk has got a weapon behind the counter or maybe the store is wired to the cop station."

"If we hit him fast and hard, he won't have time to do nothing, not pull a piece, not trigger an alarm, nothing." Eddie's tone was low and steady. That by itself told Joey that the job was going to happen. It was just a matter of when.

"We'll do it on Friday, that's when the till is flush with cash. Are you in, Joey? Don't let me down."

"Yeah, I'm in." Joey understood that he knew too much not to be in. His only other choice was to be completely out and he thought he had too much to live for. "How much do you think the take will be?"

Eddie smiled as he scratched his head and dislodged a shower of dandruff flakes. "I knew a guy who worked there three years ago. He told me that it averaged twenty grand."

"Twenty grand, you're shitting me!" Joey nearly swallowed his gum.

"Yeah, twenty grand, five from the liquor store and fifteen from two small book-making operations the owner has off-site. It all goes in the same safe under the checkout counter. Every Saturday morning, the owner, Omar, comes in to collect the receipts. He doesn't show up again until the next Saturday. Nobody has ever touched his operation before; he must have worked a deal with the cops. Three years ago, when my friend worked there, fifty grand passed through the store on super bowl weekend."

After hearing that the take was twenty grand, Joey moved from reluctantly in to all the way in. They drove back to Joey's aunt's place, a small house south of the city.

Joey's aunt was in her late seventies, nearly deaf and in terrible health due to her many years of chain smoking and drinking. She was short, feisty and she would walk with a limp when she didn't get her way and wanted to foster sympathy. By supplying her with gin and cigarettes, Joey had secured a place to stay for as long as he wanted. Eddie was able to stay there too, as long as he cleaned up after himself and helped with the grocery bills. They entered the house and went straight to Joey's room. It was Monday and they had a lot to do before Friday.

CHAPTER THREE

George and Juan had finished their shift and were heading home. "Did everything go all right back at work? The other guys in the crew aren't giving you any trouble are they?" George asked.

"No, no, everything is fine. It's okay working here. You know I want to be a cop, don't you?"

"I know," said George, "but I think they prefer being called police officers. I don't understand why you're interested in police work. Your grades were good in school, and you could be a teacher or something. We could get you into a real college, full time, when things settle down."

"I want to be a police officer, Dad, I always have. I think I'll be good at it. I know I will."

George knew it too. They rode the rest of the way home in silence, giving him time to remember why he agreed that Juan would make a good cop.

Thirteen years earlier, on George's tenth anniversary with Acme Janitorial Services, they threw him a party at a bar near work. George was a good worker and he was popular with both the janitors and the bosses, so everyone was having a genuinely good time.

After a few hours, the party started to wind down. One of the bosses offered to buy George one for the road. As the boss put on his coat and started to head toward the door, a striking blond in a red dress approached George standing at the bar. She asked him what the party was for. As he turned to answer, he caught the boss' eye. The boss gave him a wink and George assumed that he was receiving a pre-paid gift. Actually, the boss gave George a wink of admiration for talking to the blond. A few drinks and a few hours later, George woke up in an alley with a bump on his head and his pockets turned inside out.

He made it home and told his wife, Marie, most of the story. He told her the part about the party and the drinking and passing out and hitting his head. Fortunately, he didn't have much money on him, just $23, but $23 is $23. Marie let him have it just enough to voice her displeasure at his drinking too much, but not enough to create a problem for the family.

The next afternoon, George was watching the baseball game on TV with Juan, who was about four years old. Juan turned to his father and said, "Daddy, why did the lady take your money?"

George said, "You don't need to worry about that, Son. Let's go outside and play catch." Neither of them ever brought it up again. Over the years, Juan demonstrated that he knew things that he should have no way of knowing. It didn't happen often, but it did happen.

Years later, George found out that Juan had been tested in grammar school. The testing consisted of one session with the school's part-time child psychologist, Dr. Anthony Michaels.

Juan was six when he met with Dr. Michaels, a recent Brown graduate, padding his resume with this education job. Dr. Michaels was writing a book titled Early Advanced Education for the Gifted Child and he thought that he could kill two birds with the same stone by testing children for the school system, while gathering data for his book.

Juan entered the office just as the psychologist was hanging up the phone. Dr. Michaels introduced himself and Juan cheerfully said, "You have a little girl and a puppy!" Dr. Michaels was floored. "How did you know that?" he asked.

"I don't know."

"Do you know my daughter?"

"No."

"Did someone tell you that I have a little girl and a puppy?"

"No."

The questioning went on for ten minutes with no result. Juan had been right. Dr. Michaels did have a wife, a young daughter and a new Lab puppy. He looked around the office for clues to the boy's insight. It really wasn't his office, he just used it. He had no family pictures or personal items there.

Juan appeared to be a normal, bright but not gifted little boy. The questioning had made Juan defensive, so Dr. Michaels began the testing and motor skills exercises and worked to put him at ease. Juan seemed to relax and started enjoying the tests and puzzles that Dr. Michaels gave him. Then, while Juan was distracted with a 30-piece puzzle, Dr. Michaels asked, "Did you see my little girl?"

"No, I heard her."

"When did you hear her?"

"When I came into the room, she was on the phone and she said, 'Goodbye, Daddy'."

Dr. Michaels had barely heard the child say goodbye when he hung up the phone. How could Juan have heard it from across the room? It wasn't possible. "Are you bothered by loud noises and can you hear things that are far away?"

"No." Juan kept putting together the puzzle.

"Do you hear really well?"

"I guess." He put in a piece of the puzzle.

"Do you like puppies?

"Yes."

"Why did you mention that I have a puppy?"

"You smell like a puppy." Juan said.

Earlier, at home, Dr. Michaels had found the puppy he bought for his daughter wandering around the living room, so he picked him up and put him in the pen the family had constructed for him in the kitchen. He went out and got the newspaper, had a cup of coffee, read the paper and left for work.

He sniffed himself and he became aware of a non-offensive odor that did remind him of the puppy. But he was behind a desk and Juan was on the other side of the room when he mentioned the little girl and the puppy. So, both revelations could now be explained, not by supernatural abilities, but certainly exceptional ones.

Dr. Michaels had Juan close his eyes and describe the office from memory, which he did in exact detail. Dr. Michaels was elated. It appeared that Juan was gifted, maybe even a savant. If he was a savant, it was with no outward abnormalities, a very rare case.

For the rest of the session, every effort was made to befriend Juan, to praise him and to make him believe that this meeting was a reward for the good work he was doing at school. When they were done, Juan left the office and went back to class.

Dr. Michaels' head was swimming. What a find! He

could see that his book's direction, title and everything else would be changed to reflect the research he was about to do with Juan. He had to keep Juan a secret until he had more information. *Was his ability always active or did it occur in flashes? Was it triggered by stress? Having a session with a school psychologist must have been stressful. Has he always had his abilities or are they just emerging?*

He knew that he shouldn't get ahead of himself. The first thing he had to do was to get ahold of Juan's school records and any information about his family. He wanted to get prepared to meet his parents. Without parental permission, all testing and research with Juan would stop dead.

That evening over dinner, Juan told George and Marie about the fun day he had in school. He told them about the tests and the puzzles and how he was scared when Dr. Michaels asked him all those questions. Marie couldn't wait to get to school with Juan the next morning. When she found out she couldn't get an appointment to talk to Juan's teacher that morning, she went to the assistant principal's office and was able to speak to him.

After a heated discussion, with the understanding that her next stop would be the principal's office if her wishes weren't met, it was decided that since Juan had no behavioral problems, there would be no further contact with the school psychologist. Dr. Michaels was crushed and his calls and letters to the parents didn't sway them.

CHAPTER FOUR

George pulled into the driveway of his far from paid for single family, brown, four-bedroom house. "I suppose you're going to grab breakfast, get your things and head off to school now? I don't know where you get the energy. That classroom must be filled with pretty girls."

"No, Dad, I'm serious about school. Girls can come later"

"Son, girls come when they come. There's a saying. 'You can't control the timing of the beat of your heart.' At least, I think that's how that expression goes."

"Right, Dad."

Two hours later, when Juan entered the classroom and took his seat, he looked around. There were no pretty girls to speak of, just a couple of middle aged housewives and a bunch of mid-twenty looking ex military types. There were also two guys who looked like stone cold thugs.

The classroom looked like the same ones he just left in high school. The walls were painted olive green and the ceiling was white and there was a wall-to-wall sliding chalk board in the front of the room. It wasn't what he expected of a college classroom, even if this was only community college. He had envisioned large sloping lecture halls, air conditioning and plush chairs. No matter. It was only temporary.

The class looked like it might be interesting after all. In addition to the expected discussions and papers covering topics like: *What is a Crime?, What is a Criminal?, The Elements of Criminal Law, Collecting and Using Criminal Statistics etc...,* the class was going to work with case studies. And the class could discuss, not study current events. Juan knew he could suffer through all the textbook crap until they got to the good stuff.

CHAPTER FIVE

It was Friday finally, and Eddie and Joey were set to go. They had gone over the plan a hundred times and they had been clean and sober for two days now. Joey had a gun that belonged to his dad. It was a .22 that hadn't been fired for a couple of years, but he kept it clean. That gun had been his best friend in school when he was continually bullied.

When he had finally had enough of the abuse, he took his father's gun and showed it to the right people, and he was never bothered again. He didn't want to get even; he just wanted to be left alone. It was a good thing that simply showing the gun tucked in his belt was all it took to stop the harassment, because Joey was fully prepared to use it.

Eddie had to steal a car. He planned to do it right before the robbery. If he got caught, that would be the end of the job. Eddie was going to pick up the car at the hospital parking lot. He knew that hospital employees work all three shifts, so a car taken from the lot after 11:00 pm wouldn't be missed until six or seven the next morning. Eddie had worked in an auto repair shop long enough to learn how to boost cars.

The plan was simple, Joey would enter the store, avoiding the security camera and go to the back of the store. He would break something and call the clerk for assistance. When the clerk went to help, Eddie would enter the store, go behind the counter and get the clerk's piece. Then they would force him to open the cash register and the safe. They'd take the money, put plastic ties on his wrists and ankles, and duct tape his mouth. They should be in and out in five minutes. They'd go back to the hospital, pick up their car and go back to Joey's place. They were going to lay low for a few days, no partying, no big spending. They thought the plan was perfect.

Joey had slipped a sedative in his aunt's gin so she'd be asleep while they were gone. If they needed an alibi, she would vouch for them. They were careful leaving the house, no unusual lights on, no noise. They had even parked the car down the block so no one would hear it when it started up after midnight. They drove to the hospital.

"Are you sure getting the car ain't gonna be a problem?" asked Joey.

"Just wait and see."

"No car, no caper." Joey secretly hoped that Eddie had exaggerated his ability to boost cars.

"Shut up and watch!"

They entered the parking lot, and Eddie spotted the car he wanted, a 1992 Pontiac Firebird Grand Prix. He didn't want any part of the newer cars with their 'On Star' and theft deterrent gadgets. He parked at the end of the row in what looked like a security camera blind spot, ten cars away from the target. They walked to the Firebird; Eddie pulled out a slip-stick and used it to open the car door in three seconds. Then he reached under the steering wheel, pulled and twisted the ignition wires and the car started up.

Joey was impressed and disappointed. The caper was on and he had better do his part. Eddie wanted to drive around for a few minutes to see if they got away without being spotted, but he couldn't take the chance. They had no lights, one of the drawbacks of bypassing the ignition switch. Eddie drove straight to the liquor store, set the hand brake and kept the motor running. Joey was sweating and breathing heavy. They sat in the car looking around. The parking lot was empty and the store looked empty, except for the clerk behind the counter. It was showtime.

CHAPTER SIX

Azlan, the store clerk, was 27. He was six feet tall, with a slight but muscular build, jet-black hair and an infectious smile. He could even be described as handsome. He had come to this country on a student visa in 2003 and never made it past the second semester at Cal Northridge. He was Omar's distant cousin, and he was given a job and a place to stay. Omar didn't pay Azlan well, but he paid him regularly, which was fine. Azlan didn't have that much to do, working the 10:00 pm to 6:00 am shift. He cleaned up the store, stocked merchandise and handled the cash register. Whenever there was more than $2000 in the cash register, he transferred $1500 to the safe.

He loved being in this country. His success with the friendly, uninhibited, seemingly endless supply of young ladies in the city made his decision to stay an easy one. He got along well with Omar and the men who worked for him by simply doing what he was told and always showing them respect. He knew his boss was an important man who owned several businesses in the area. He owned the apartment building in which Azlan had a small, rent-free apartment. Omar also had many close political ties back home.

Azlan hadn't opened the safe since just after 10:30 pm when he got a delivery. Every once in a while, during Azlan's shift, Omar got special deliveries at the store. Usually it was a small package or an envelope that Azlan had to put in the safe. The people making the deliveries didn't wear brown shirts and shorts. This night, a man came in the store and handed Azlan an envelope and said, "This is a special delivery for Omar." That was it. There were no questions asked and no receipts given.

It was just after 1:00 am, and Azlan had taken in almost $1200. Added to what was in the cash register when he started his shift, he had $2100. He was transferring cash to the safe when a small, hooded man came in the store and quickly walked to the back. Suddenly, there were crashing sounds at the back of the store and Azlan grabbed the wooden club he kept behind the counter and ran toward the noise. As he reached Joey, Eddie came through the door and ran behind the counter. Azlan looked at Eddie, turned back to Joey and raised his club. A startled Joey pulled his gun, fired and said, "Hold it!"

Azlan was hit in the neck. The arterial spray caught Joey's sleeve and right pant leg. Azlan grabbed his neck and screamed something neither of the robbers understood. He spun around, falling against a shelf, but he stayed on his feet and started to run toward the entrance. Joey fired again; the bullet hit Azlan high on his shoulder and knocked him off balance. He fell to the floor, still holding his neck, making guttural sounds and blowing blood bubbles. In an instant, they were on him, trying to secure him with the plastic ties.

Azlan was weak and in shock and they were able to get his hands behind his back and put on the ties. Eddie ran back behind the counter and emptied the cash register, putting the money in a pillowcase that he brought with him. He turned to leave and saw the safe was ajar. He emptied the safe, taking cash, papers, everything. There was a small TV/VCR combination under the counter and he popped the tape and put it in the pillowcase. Joey was standing in the doorway.

"Come on, let's go!"

Eddie went to the door and looked back to see that

Azlan had stopped moving. Then he ran out.

It took everything that Eddie had to hold the car's speed under 40. He took a direct route back to the hospital. He parked the car in what he thought was the same space. They got back in their car and Joey drove them home.

Joey's aunt was still out cold. They were covered with blood, Joey especially. Putting on the plastic ties didn't go as smoothly as planned. "Why'd ya haf ta shoot him, you idiot?" Eddie shouted.

"Keep your voice down. He was going to brain me with that bat. I did what I had to do. It's too late to worry about it now. Let's just do what we got to do."

Eddie was pissed, but he knew Joey was right. They stripped, showered and washed their clothes using bleach. Joey put on shorts and a tee shirt and went out to the car with a bucket of soapy bleach water and worked on the seats and floor. The gun had to go, but they'd wait until daylight to get rid of it. They scrubbed their shoes with soap and water. And when they couldn't think of anything else to do, they argued about the mistakes they made and drank themselves to sleep.

CHAPTER SEVEN

At 6:45 am nurse Ellen Porter was relieved from her shift early by the new girl, who was trying to score points with a cute intern by putting in as much face time as she could when he was working. Nurse Porter was tired and happy to be going home. She left the building and breathed in the warm, fresh morning air as she walked to her car. The car wasn't in her usual parking spot. She got in and tried the key but nothing happened. She turned the key again. No luck. She noticed the copper smell and saw the large chocolate colored stain on the passenger seat. She knew it was blood. She saw the ignition wires dangling under the steering wheel and she quickly got out of the car. She grabbed her cell phone and dialed 911.

"911. What is the nature of your emergency?"

"My car has been vandalized and there's blood on the seats."

"What is your name and location, please?"

"My name is Ellen Porter; I'm a nurse at Saint Mary's Hospital. I'm in the hospital parking lot near the Greenwood Avenue entrance."

"Stay on the line. I'm dispatching a car to your location."

A patrol car arrived five minutes later. The officers collected as much information as they could. It appeared that the car was stolen, damaged and returned. The blood on the seat concerned the officers. They arranged to have the car impounded and looked at by the Crime Lab technicians. Nurse Porter was told to call her insurance company.

Omar arrived at the liquor store a few minutes after 7:00 am. He expected the lights to be out and the door to be locked. He pushed the door open and looked around. He spotted Azlan on the floor in the center aisle. He could see the large pool of blood around his head. His eyes were wide open and vacant. Omar ran behind the counter and saw that the safe was open and empty. He walked to the front of the store and locked the door.

He made a call on his cell phone while walking to the office in the back of the store. He finished his phone call and sat down at his desk. He started to make a list of everything of value that was in the safe. It took him 2 minutes to finish the list. Money was not one of the items listed.

He walked back to the body and looked at it and said, "Azlan, my friend, I will find who did this and they will be punished."

Omar was careful not to get any blood on himself. He was a stout man just under six feet tall, with thinning hair and a round face. He looked completely non-threatening except for his eyes. His eyes were almost black and had a chilling effect on whomever they targeted. Omar had been a soldier and he had seen many bodies before. He stood there unemotionally surveying the scene, "Sloppy, very sloppy."

Twenty minutes later, there was a knock at the back door. Omar went to the window that faced the back alley and peered out. He opened the door for Hassan and Anwar. Omar pointed them to Azlan's body and told them to clean up the mess and remove the body. They looked at each other and Omar repeated the order. They didn't ask for an explanation, they just started to do what they were told. Omar walked back to the office and made another call.

"Whoever this is, this better be good."

"Detective Morrison, this is Omar. I've got a problem. The store got hit last night and one of my guys got killed."

"Did you call it in?"

"No I'm cleaning it up myself and I want you to handle it."

"I can't do anything on my own; the whole force has to be involved. The ME, Forensics, the Crime Scene guys, everyone has to get involved."

"I just want you to point me in the right direction; I have my own people who can handle the heavy lifting. Whoever did this wasn't a pro, the place is a mess. It was a very sloppy kill."

"Okay, I'll do what I can. Before you clean the place up, take some pictures. I'm going to need something to work with."

Omar said, "Sure thing, I got to go." He ended the call and ran to the front of the store yelling "Stop!"

Hassan and Anwar had spent the last two minutes planning the cleanup and very little had been done.

"Stop! Don't do anything yet, I want to get some pictures of the body and the scene for our policeman friend. He will find who did this and you two will avenge Azlan."

Anwar and Hassan nodded in agreement. Then Omar sent Anwar to the local hardware store for plastic tarps to line the back of the liquor store's van. He told Hassan to pick up the merchandise that had been knocked off the shelves without disturbing the area around the body. And he went home to get his camera.

CHAPTER EIGHT

Eddie woke up with wicked a hangover. He could smell the coffee Joey's aunt had made. It looked like she had made coffee and breakfast for herself and gone back to her room to watch her TV. *"Thank goodness for the 24-hour Soap Channel,"* he mumbled.

He poured himself a cup of coffee and settled into a kitchen chair. Thinking about what a mess the robbery turned out to be made him shake his head in disgust. All of a sudden, he stiffened and he sat up straight in the chair. He realized that they hadn't yet counted the money.

He went to Joey's room and woke him up. If they counted the money, they had better do it together. It made no sense to create problems between them now. They opened the pillowcase and dumped the contents on the bed. There were bundles of cash and loose papers and an envelope. They counted eighteen thousand five hundred dollars in small bills. They were thrilled at their good fortune. Most of the papers weren't in English, so they were ignored. The ones that were in English were written in legalese, so they were ignored as well. Eddie grabbed the envelope and tore it open. There was a sheet of paper with a series of letters and numbers. There were several rows of characters on the page.

"Let's get rid of all this stuff," said Joey.

"Naw, these things may be worth some money to the right people."

"How are we gonna find out who the right people are?"

"I don't know. Maybe Omar will want to buy his stuff back after things cool down. Let's just sit on this stuff for a while. We can figure out what to do with it later."

Joey agreed, "But we got to get rid of the gun and the videotape and our clothes too. They didn't wash clean."

"All right, we'll burn the videotape and dump the gun and clothes."

"You want to watch it first?" asked Joey.

"Naw, let's just fire up the barbeque and get rid of it."

CHAPTER NINE

Bonnie Rupp turned over in bed and looked at the alarm clock. It was 8:45 am. She hoped Azlan would be home long before this. She expected to have a couple of hours with him before she had to go to work. Bonnie and Azlan had been seeing each other for two months; it wasn't serious, it was just fun. Last week, Azlan gave her a key to his apartment for emergencies and since then, Bonnie discovered the need for emergency sex twice.

They had met at the restaurant that Bonnie managed downtown. Azlan was there with a date who introduced him. Bonnie was blond and five feet six and a half inches tall, and a hundred and thirty pounds. She was beautiful, and he liked her looks, but he was more impressed with her poise and her in-charge attitude. She commanded respect and she got it from everyone who worked at the restaurant. Azlan had never met any woman like Bonnie. He wanted to dump his date and go after her, but he played it cool. He smiled politely, met his server, ate his meal and enjoyed his evening, all the while discretely stealing glances at the restaurant manager whenever he could. Bonnie was aware of the attention Azlan was paying her. When he showed up a day later alone, she knew they were going to be together.

Bonnie decided that she couldn't wait for Azlan any longer; she just had time to run home to her own apartment, check the mail and run a few errands before going to work. She'd call later to find out why he didn't show up. She showered, dressed, locked up and ran out.

CHAPTER TEN

Omar finished taking pictures of everything that appeared to be significant. He even went behind the counter and shot pictures of the partially open safe. He looked at Azlan's TV/VCR combo and poked the VCR slot. The machine was empty. Omar knew that Azlan watched movies during his shift when there was nothing else to do. He had rigged the TV to accept the security camera feed when the VCR wasn't operating and play the movie tape when the VCR was in use. "Those ass-holes took the tape," he said to himself. "Why would those sons of a dog take...?" He realized that the robbers must have thought that they were taking the surveillance tape. The security tape was actually recorded on a machine in the office. "What an idiot. I forgot about the security system."

Omar went to the office, opened the cabinet and pressed 'stop' then 'rewind' on the recording machine. He backed up to 1:10 am and started playing the tape. Azlan was sitting behind the counter counting money. Omar fast-forwarded the tape. At 1:38 am a man in a hood came in the store, a minute later Azlan got up and ran to the back of the store. Another man came in the store and went behind the counter, then he ran to the back of the store. There was no sound on the tape. Next, Omar saw all three men struggling. Azlan was gushing blood from his face or neck. They tied his hands and feet. One of the robbers ran behind the counter and emptied the cash register, then he went under the counter to the safe. He kept his head down, avoiding the security camera. He started to leave, then stopped and looked at

Azlan's TV, and then up to the security camera and smiled. He took Azlan's tape and left.

Omar took out his cell phone.

"This is Detective Morrison speaking."

"This is Omar. I took the pictures. But better still, I've got security footage of the crime. There is a good shot of one of the punks."

"Great. I'm tied up until lunchtime. I'll be there at one o'clock to have a look."

"Good. The store will be cleaned up by then. This should simplify things for you. I just need you to ID the guy and get me an address. I'll do the rest."

"I'll see you this afternoon."

Morrison knew that it still wasn't going to be easy to identify a guy from a security tape. The way it's normally done is to get the news media to work for you, ask the public. He had to do this all on his own in his spare time. He had to give it a shot; it was not a good idea to disappoint Omar. He would make up a list of bad guys who targeted convenience and liquor stores. Then he'd get a still shot of the perp on the tape and show it around. He was aware that a lot of these bad guys knew each other and they didn't like competition.

Fortunately, he was partnered up with Detective Ann Howard, probably because no one else wanted her. *"Diversity in action"*, he thought to himself. As long as he was partnered with Howard, getting these little, off the books investigations done wasn't a problem. She didn't have a clue, but she was a good lay, the one time they did it. Morrison scribbled a note on his desk pad to see Omar at 1:00 pm. Morrison was medium height and a little on the heavy side. The hair he had left was starting to turn from brown to gray and his most distinguishing feature was his glasses with their small round frames that made him look like a high school teacher. He had lied to Omar about being tied up. His morning was free and he looked at the overnight incident reports. It had been a slow night, a purse snatching, three reports of stolen cars, a residential burglary and a bar fight.

He had a thought, "*The perps would have stolen a car to commit the robbery.*" He looked at the stolen car incident reports again. One report stood out. The car, a 1992 Pontiac Firebird, was found with blood on the seat. Omar had said that the store was a real mess after the robbery. According to the report, the car had been impounded and the lab boys were scheduled to look it over.

If the lab pulled any usable prints from the car, Omar's little job would be a piece of cake. The prints would ID the perps and no legwork would be necessary. Morrison called Mac Archer, the officer who would normally be in charge of a stolen car case, and he asked to be kept informed of any developments. Morrison lied that he had a case that might possible overlap, but he assured the officer that any collar would be his. Now, all Morrison had to do was to wait.

Eddie and Joey watched the local news channel. There was no news about a homicide or robbery at the liquor store. It didn't make sense. The crime must have been discovered by now. Eddie figured that the newspapers couldn't get the story until the late edition or the next morning, but the TV news was usually Johnny on the spot. They were tempted to drive by the store to have a look, but they thought better of it and stayed away. They only left the house to dump the gun and their shoes in Clear Lake on the Australian Avenue side, and they also put their clothes and shoes in a church dumpster about two miles from the house. They spent the rest of the morning and most of the afternoon watching the news. They couldn't have missed the story if it was broadcasted. Something was very wrong.

Bonnie called Azlan's apartment twice and got the answering machine. She left a message the first time, not the second. *"Where the hell can he be? This is not like him."* She remembered that she had only known Azlan for two months and really didn't know that much about him. She knew that he lied to her about owning the liquor store where he worked. She found that out from Azlan's date, the woman who introduced them. Bonnie went back to work annoyed. An hour later, she called again, first the apartment and then the store.

"Hello. This is Bonnie Rupp, a friend of Azlan's. Is he there?"

"No, he left before I arrived this morning."

"Well, he didn't come home after work and I haven't been able to reach him all day. I'm beginning to worry."

"I'm sure he is all right. He does have relatives in the area, maybe he's visiting one of them," said Omar.

"Okay, but if you see him, will you tell him I called?"

"Of course. Bonnie is it? Maybe you'd better leave your number just in case."

"All right, it's 876-4526."

"I'll tell him you called. Goodbye"

"Goodbye!"

Omar was pissed. *"Oh great, a girlfriend. When Azlan doesn't call, she'll cause trouble."*

She was a loose end. He was going to have to find out everything he could about her.

It was 1:10 pm when Detective Ken Morrison arrived. "You're late!" yelled Omar.

"I had things do on my real job. Let's have a look at that tape."

Omar walked Morrison to the office and they watched the tape. "You're right, those guys are definitely amateurs. That headshot is good. I'll take a picture of that and show it around."

"Be quick about it. These guys need to be found soon. You might as well know, there were some sensitive papers in the safe. I need them back, the sooner the better."

"I'll do my best."

"Another thing, here is the telephone number for a Bonnie Rump or Rubb. Find out where she lives, and everything you can about her."

"Who's she?"

"She was Azlan's girlfriend. I don't want her asking questions."

"I'll take care of it. By the way, I'm going to need an advance this week."

"Fine," said Omar as he took a roll of bills from his pocket and peeled off ten twenty-dollar bills. "Make sure you find these guys quick."

Morrison got the still picture, left the store and headed

to his car. Outside, in front of the store, Morrison looked around. He saw that there was a security camera in the parking lot of the strip mall across the street. He crossed the street and went in the mall. He flashed his badge as he entered the security office in the five-store mall. It was more like a security closet. The guard's desk took up half the floor space.

The guard was tall and trim. He looked to be in his early sixties. The security camera was working and the tapes were kept for two weeks, then reused. Morrison had the guard back up the tape to 1:30 am. On the tape, a dark Pontiac Firebird parked near the liquor store at 1:35 am and took off in a hurry at 1:44 am. He couldn't see the license plate. Morrison thanked the guard and left.

He really had no intention of showing the still picture around town. If he did ask around and a week later the guy in question showed up dead, he'd have to start coming up with answers.

At half past five, Hassan and Anwar left the store, having been relieved by Aalia and Hushni, a married couple, who thought they ran the store for a Holding Company and were working their way to full ownership. According to the paperwork filed with the city, Aalia and Hushni did own the store.

Hassan and Anwar drove the van toward the interstate, planning to dump Azlan's body in the Wetlands State Park twenty miles northwest of the city. They were pissed that they had to work the day shift at the store and then get rid of the body. Dumping the body was nothing. The real objection was to selling liquor. They were soldiers, not clerks. This work was beneath them. And the fact that a man like Azlan was killed protecting bottles of alcohol was almost too much to bear. "Omar will find the dogs that killed Azlan," said Hassan. "When they're found, I hope they resist."

"They stole documents that Omar needs, and we will get them back," said Anwar smiling. "We will get them back."

The dumpsite was deep in the woods and they were prepared for the terrain by bringing their combat boots and fatigues. They drove in the backwoods as far as they could, then they changed clothes and took the body out of the van. They carried Azlan's body a hundred yards further into the thicket and removed the plastic tarp. The body had been stripped of everything. They dug a shallow grave and buried the body with as much dignity as the circumstances allowed.

Eddie and Joey watched the eleven o'clock news from beginning to end, even the commercials. There was no word on the shooting. The crime was being covered up. Their minds were running at full speed. Eddie was thinking out loud. "Either the cops know about it and are investigating with a media blackout, or the crime was never reported."

They couldn't come up with any reason the cops would want to keep it quiet. After a minute, Joey said, "The liquor store owner must not have reported the crime. Maybe the owner doesn't want anyone to know that the store clerk died."

"No, that can't be it. The owner doesn't want anyone to know there was a robbery. He'd have to answer questions about what was taken. The papers must be more important than a robbery and a homicide. Maybe the papers were worth some real money."

Eddie was too tired to think about it and the drinking didn't help. One thing was clear. This was good news. If the crime wasn't reported, the cops weren't looking for them. They were home free.

CHAPTER ELEVEN

Juan started his shift on time as usual. With his Dad as his ride, there was no chance of being late for work. He cleaned the interrogation rooms and the restrooms. He almost forgot that he wanted to see if anyone noticed what he had done. He didn't consider it a big deal. But, in class, they would have called it interfering with an active investigation. Juan entered the Detective Squad, and worked his way to the conference room. Next to his little prank he saw:

Doctor affair?   Laura Sample 328 Waverly Pl.
Registered gun owner

They were pulling his leg. Someone must have seen him write on the whiteboard and now they were messing with him. They had him. He couldn't say anything without admitting to writing the note. He was tempted to put something else on the board, but he thought he'd better not. He had learned his lesson. From now on, he'd leave things alone and keep his ideas to himself.

The story broke in the Monday morning papers. "Doctor and Mistress Indicted for Killing Wife". Juan was blown away. It wasn't a gag. Someone had looked at his hint on the board and ran with it. They found out about the affair, looked at the mistress and solved the case.

"Was it just luck?" Juan wondered. *"Maybe there was something in the room that pointed to a mistress and I was the only*

one who could see it. But I didn't see it, I guessed it." Juan was in a daze. In his mind, he went over everything he could remember about the murder case. He was surprised that he could remember as much as he did. He remembered a note on the lead detective's desk that said that the doctor knew of his wife's affair. It was just logical to expect the doctor to have his own affair. Juan smiled as he looked around, making sure no one heard him say, "I solved my first case."

Bonnie had been calling Azlan's apartment all weekend with no luck. She was fed up. She wanted to know that he was okay, even if he was shacked up with somebody else. Bonnie called the police and was told to come down to the station and fill out a missing persons report. She agreed to take care of the report on her way home from work. She hoped Azlan would surface somewhere before the end of her shift.

In addition to working at the store on Saturday and dumping his body, Hassan was told to search Azlan's apartment to make sure that nothing was there that shouldn't be. Omar paid the utilities at the place so nothing was in Azlan Yardim's name. Hassan did a thorough search. He found Azlan's Glock, case, and extra magazine, and nothing else.

Hassan held the gun and thought that things would have been different if Azlan had his side arm with him that night. Azlan was good with a gun, but Omar didn't want any guns at the store for any reason. No attention was to be focused on the store or the people who worked there. To Omar's way of thinking, if you used a gun in the store, you had better have a license to carry it. If you didn't, you'd be the one being investigated.

"Stupid policy," Hassan said as he finished his search. "Every liquor store in the country has a piece behind the counter. Damn Omar." He nervously looked around to make sure he was alone when he cursed Omar.

Hassan noticed that the phone answering machine light was blinking. He pressed the button and a mechanical voice said, "You have fourteen messages." Hassan pressed the play button and the answering machine played two messages and twelve hang-ups. In the first message, a woman on the phone said, "Azlan, this is Bonnie, I missed you this morning. Call me."

In the last message, the woman said, "Shit, pick up. The hell with this, I'm calling the police!"

The cell phone call to Omar was brief. Hassan was to pack Azlan's things and make it look like he left in a hurry and might not come back. It was a furnished apartment and Azlan had no pictures or personal items other that his clothes and jewelry. Hassan packed everything in two suitcases and left.

Detective Morrison was looking at the stolen car report when Omar called.

"Do you have anything on the girlfriend?"

"Yeah. Her name is Bonnie Rupp; she's the manager at the Three Flames restaurant. She works 11:00 am to 2:00 pm and 5:00 pm to 10:00 pm and she lives at 785 Village Boulevard, apartment 4C."

"Do you need anything else on the girl?" Morrison

asked.

"No, that's all for now."

"What are you going to do?"

"I'll give her an explanation for his disappearance. If she's smart, she'll be satisfied and back off. If not, she'll join him."

"Think it through," said Morrison. "People go missing all the time. The missing person guys make two phone calls and file the case away. But if a second person goes missing, other people get involved, people who don't stop looking. Play it cool, don't do anything drastic."

"I see your point. Do you have any information about the two gentlemen I want to find?"

"Not yet, it might take a little time."

"Make it soon!" Omar hung up. He was disappointed that one of the options for dealing with the girl had been taken away. It was 11:15 am. Omar called information and got the number for the Three Flames. After holding for three minutes, Bonnie came on the line.

"Hello, this is Bonnie."

"Hello, this is Azlan's boss from the liquor store. He asked me to call you."

"How is he? Is he all right? Why didn't he call himself?"

"He's fine. He wanted me to tell you that he was leaving the country and returning home. He said there were family problems at home and his Visa has expired anyway so he's leaving. He stopped at the store to pick up his check and he left. He said he was sorry that he couldn't tell you goodbye in person."

"Did he leave a number or an address where I can reach him?"

"No, that's all the information I have, sorry."

"I can't believe he left without saying goodbye. Thank you for letting me know."

"Goodbye," said Omar, pleased that the loose end was no more.

"Goodbye." Bonnie hung up shaking her head in disbelief. *"I know I meant more to him than this. Azlan was a romantic. He would have found a way to say goodbye so that I would always remember him."* This wasn't right. She planned to file the missing persons report anyway.

CHAPTER TWELVE

Eddie and Joey were hung over after a weekend of partying hard. If nobody was looking for them, then why lay low? They didn't want to attract any attention to themselves, but they didn't have to be hermits. They had their weekend fun as cheaply as possible. Only well drinks, no champagne, no fancy dinners. They had a great time and only spent two hundred dollars. They washed up and put on their new tee shirts and jeans. It was just past noon and they were on their way to Denny's for breakfast.

"I've been thinking," said Eddie. "If the crime wasn't reported, someone wanted to cover up the loss of the cash and papers, right?" He continued on before Joey could respond, "The cash and papers are more important than the clerk's life. No, it can't be the cash, it's just the papers. They don't want the papers made public."

"I've been thinking too. There's nothing on the news about a robbery or a death. There's no report of a body being found."

"Yeah, whoever covered this up knew what they were doing."

"If the papers are so important, maybe they are looking for us. And if they can cover up a crime and get rid of a body, maybe they can find us on their own," said Joey.

"Hey, we're okay, they got no security tape, no witnesses, no nothing."

"We could take the cash, hop in the car and go

wherever we want."

"We got no need to run, and I got no place to go. Let's put the papers in a locker at the bus station and just lay low. "

Eddie pretended to be unconcerned, but Joey made a good point. He wondered who could cover up the crime and get away with it. He thought that there could be a mob connection to the liquor store; and if there was, running wasn't going to help. He was glad that they had gotten away clean.

It was 4:00 pm and Bonnie was headed for the police station to file the missing persons report. *'If Azlan did leave the country, the police should have a way of verifying it.'* She drove past the liquor store and was tempted to stop in, but she changed her mind. It was in a bad neighborhood and there was something seedy about the place.

She thought, "*Maybe this is how he breaks off relationships?*" She knew that they really weren't in a relationship, more like friends with benefits. She thought that the friendship had almost run its course and was considering ending it.

She entered the station and walked up to the receptionist's desk and got directions to Missing Persons. "*A receptionist in a police station?*" she thought to herself. "*Guess it's cheaper than having a real officer man that desk.*"

She gave her information to a young female officer who was more interested in her relationship to the missing person than the person himself. It was embarrassing for Bonnie to admit how much she didn't know about Azlan. She couldn't answer questions about next of kin, country of origin, resident status, etc. The officer was wondering if Azlan Yardim even belonged in this country. Bonnie felt like a fool. She left the station wishing that she hadn't bothered.

Upstairs in the station, Detective Morrison was on the phone being told that the 1992 Pontiac Firebird had been processed.

"There was only one set of usable prints. The prints belonged to an Edward Donovan. Donovan has a rap sheet for petty theft, purse snatching, breaking and entering, and auto theft. He has no known address, no next of kin. There were no drops of blood or spatter in the car and the theory was that the blood was transferred and the perp may not have been the injured person. Donovan or Eddie, as he liked to be called, spent six months in the county jail for assault. He was released five weeks ago and he has seven known associates. I'll send you the list."

"That's not exactly the road map I was looking for," said Morrison, "but thanks. If you find out anything else like where to find this dirt bag, let me know." He hung up. *"I've got his picture and his name. If any of the known associates are local and out on the street, I'll be in business. I guess there's some leg work to be done after all."*

CHAPTER THIRTEEN

Juan was not surprised to see the mess in the detective squad lunchroom. Confetti and streamers were everywhere. *"It must have been a heck of a party. I should have been here."* He was glad the case had been solved, but a little upset about not getting any of the credit. Then again, maybe he didn't deserve any of the credit.

Juan worked hard until break-time. The mess in the lunchroom put him about ten minutes behind schedule. He took his break in the conference room. As he suspected, the detectives had moved on to the next case. The pictures on the conference room walls showed a new crime scene from every angle. This one was a home invasion robbery and homicide. The victims were an elderly couple, Don and Roberta Garrett, and their maid, Rosa.

The back door had been forced open and the security alarm had not been set. The maid had been tied and gagged, beaten badly and strangled. Mrs. Garrett had also been tied up and beaten. The couple had been shot. The maid had been with the wealthy couple for ten years. There was a safe in the house that had been opened. Cash and jewelry were missing.

According to the couple's insurance agent, over four hundred thousand dollars worth of jewelry was taken. The couple was known to have thousands in cash in the house. The neighbors didn't hear any gunshots, but they heard a car with a muffler problem leaving the house at around 9:00 pm.

The theory of the crime was, of course, robbery and the crooks tied and beat the women until Don Garrett opened the safe. Then all three were killed. Juan finished his shift a few minutes late. He explained to his waiting Dad that cleaning up the lunchroom celebration mess was the reason he was late. Juan was happy because the first case had been solved.

The next afternoon, detective Morrison got the list of Eddie Donovan's known associates from Mac Archer in Auto Theft. Five were local. Of the five locals, four were out on the street. *"This shouldn't be too bad,"* he said to himself. *"I'll get Omar off my back by the end of the day."*

"Hey Ann, I'm going down to the courthouse to sit in on a proceeding about an old drug bust. You want to come?"

"No, thank you," said Howard. "I've got some paperwork to finish up."

Morrison knew his partner wouldn't go anywhere near a courtroom by choice. Ever since her divorce case, she wanted nothing to do with lawyers or judges. Morrison locked his desk and left. He thought about telephoning Eddie's four known associates. But one of them might tip off Eddie and since he just committed a murder, he would probably take off running. Morrison had to talk to Eddie's friends face to face.

He got no answer at the first house. A neighbor told him that the young man had a warehouse job and was probably at work. He showed Eddie's picture to the neighbor. No luck. At Morrison's second stop, the home of Estelle Adams, things turned out better. Ms. Adams was home alone, but she recognized her nephew's friend Eddie, when she was shown the picture. "Yeah, Eddie is staying here. He doesn't pay me no rent, but he chips in on the grocery bills."

"My name is Ben Johnson. I've been trying to locate Mr. Donovan. He's one of the beneficiaries named in his late grandfather's will. Do you have any idea when he'll be back?"

"They come and go as they please, but they are always home for dinner."

"Thank you. I'll come back later."

Morrison called Omar from the car. "I got them. They are staying at 738 Westgate Avenue. They're not here at the moment, but they are expected back before long. I'll sit on the house until your people get here. After that, it's up to you." Twenty minutes later, Hassan and Anwar pulled up and parked across the street. Morrison nodded at them and took off.

"Omar wants them alive, both of them." Hassan hoped they would try to resist capture. The thought of Azlan bleeding to death at the hands of these two dogs haunted him. "Alive, but not necessarily unharmed."

After two hours of waiting in silence, Anwar and Hassan watched Joey and Eddie park a few doors down from the house. They got out of their car and were laughing about something. Hassan and Anwar were on Eddie and Joey in an instant. Hassan pointed his gun at Joey's head and said, "You're coming with us, both of you or I will kill you where you stand." The look in Hassan's eyes was enough to insure their cooperation. The two frightened punks got in the gunmen's car without protesting. Anwar drove and Hassan sat behind the driver and covered the two captives, one in the front passenger seat and the other in the back. "What's this all about?" Joey asked.

"Shut up! I won't tell you again." Hassan raised his gun and the captives saw that it was fitted with a silencer.

Joey was sweating and he started breathing heavily. Neither he nor Eddie was blindfolded. He realized that the guys with the guns didn't care what they saw because they were going to be dead.

After a short drive, Anwar pulled into a garage behind an apartment building. Eddie and Joey were taken into the building, then to an apartment in the basement. They entered the apartment and were directed to sit on a couch in the living room. A heavyset man in his late thirties entered the room. "You have something of mine."

"You've got the wrong guys," said Joey. Omar and Hassan exchanged a glance and Hassan shot Joey in the kneecap. Joey screamed and passed out. Eddie freaked. "Please don't hurt me. Okay, okay, we've got your money, we'll give it back."

"I want everything back."

"Okay, the money's at the house and the papers are in a locker at the bus station downtown."

"Where's the key?"

"It's back at the house. I'll go get it and bring it to you," said Eddie. "Joey can stay here with you and I'll go home, get the money and the key and come back."

"If I let you go, I'll never see you again. You'll leave your friend here to die and you'll run like a rabbit."

"No, no, trust me I'll be back."

"I know you'll be back. My man will go with you."

"No, if I give you the key, you'll kill me," said Eddie.

"I just want my property back. I don't need to kill you. Killing you will bring a lot of heat and stir up trouble. If I let you live, what can you do? You can't go to the police. You've committed a robbery and a murder. You'll go away for life, if they don't give you the needle. Now you and my man will get the money and the key, go to the bus station, get my property, and bring it back to me. While you're gone, we'll patch up your friend here, who accidently shot himself in the knee while cleaning his gun."

"I don't know."

"Know this. You will do what I ask now while you have two good legs, or ..." Omar looked at Hassan who leveled his gun at Eddie's knee.

"Okay, okay, I'll get your stuff."

"You'd better come back with everything."

"I will, I will. Please, just take care of Joey."

"Your friend will be fine. Now go!" Omar stepped aside and Eddie and Anwar left.

Omar walked over to Hassan and said, "Be patient. When they come back, you can take the two thieves to visit Azlan and put two each in the back of their heads." Hassan smiled for the first time since the robbery.

An hour and twenty minutes later, Anwar and Eddie returned to the basement apartment with the stolen documents and what was left of the stolen money. Omar carefully looked at the papers and made sure everything had been returned. The envelope that he had to have was there, but it had been opened. Omar examined the codes in the envelope. Then he said, "Take these two out in the woods somewhere and let them go."

Eddie was relieved to hear that they were going to be freed. He helped Joey back to the car with Hassan and Anwar close behind, guns drawn. They pulled out of the garage and drove toward the interstate. "How far are we going?" asked Eddie.

"Shut up! You are lucky to be alive. You robbed us and killed one of our men. And now you're worried about how far you'll have to hitchhike to get back home tonight. I should put one in your knee for the fun of it."

It took them thirty-five minutes to reach Wetlands State Park. They drove to the remote area that they had visited the day before. They walked Eddie and Joey into the woods about thirty yards from the road. Hassan and Anwar left the two thieves face down in the dirt after saying their final goodbyes.

CHAPTER FOURTEEN

Juan's opinion of the city detectives plummeted when he entered the conference room at the 4th Street Station and discovered that they hadn't made any appreciable progress on the high priority murder case. The cops were looking at the Garrett's business associates and anyone who knew that large sums were routinely kept in the house.

Juan looked at the picture of the maid tied, gagged and strangled. Juan stepped closer to the picture on the wall. *"Her murder was personal,"* he said to himself. *"The detectives must have seen that. The bad guys wanted the loot, but they wanted to kill the maid too. It must have been the maid's ex or boyfriend who did this."*

He looked on the walls and the detectives' desks to find any evidence that his theory had been looked at and discarded. One of the detectives had left his note pad on the top of his desk and had gone home.

"These guys need a security seminar." Juan found notes indicating that the maid, Rosa Torres, was a church going, widowed mother with two teenage kids. There was no mention of a new love interest. *"Maybe nobody asked or they asked and nobody knew. My theory still holds."*

Juan cleaned the offices while turning the case over and over in his mind. *"There's no ex, but maybe a boyfriend that nobody knows about. The teenage kids might not notice their mom acting like a woman in love. Teenage kids ignore their parents. But, a boyfriend couldn't stay hidden from her family for long. The family is always around. Someone would have eventually seen him."*

The notes indicated that Rosa's phone records had been checked and her calls could be explained. *"How could there be a boyfriend who wasn't seen and wasn't called? How could they be together without her family or friends seeing him?"* Juan looked around him. Except for having lunch with his dad, Juan would spend eight hours with no family or friends around. *"She was with him at work!"*

The household staff included a gardener, Luis, and a part-time chauffeur, Paul, both of whom had weak alibis. The gardener was at home alone. The chauffeur was off the day of the murder and he was shopping at the local mall. The gardener had been eliminated as a suspect because he was 64 years old. It had to be the chauffeur. There were no calls from Rosa to the chauffeur, but were there calls from the Garrett house to him?

Rosa could have called Paul from the house and saved message units on her cell phone. It fits; Paul was familiar with the house and the family's wealth. The robbers were probably masked, but Paul might be afraid that Rosa could still identify him, so he had her gagged. From the beating that Rosa was given, the love affair was probably one sided. The cops hadn't eliminated Paul, but they weren't looking at him. Juan had to leave another clue to get them on the right track. He approached the whiteboard and picked up a marker with his left hand. He wrote:

Rosa and Paul relationship?

Juan thought about the brutality of the crime and he added:

Chauffeur priors?

His additions looked inconspicuous among the many

loosely connected ideas randomly written on the board. He wasn't that confident in the detectives' powers of observation anyway.

CHAPTER FIFTEEN

The missing persons report for Azlan Yardim was edited and entered into the police incident report database. Weekly, an update file was stripped from the database and input to a batch file merge for the FBI National Missing Persons (FBINMP) file. Also weekly, when the merged FBINMP file was received in DC, it was compared to the Homeland Security Persons of High Interest list. The name Azlan Yardim was red flagged.

Six years ago when Azlan entered the country, his three months of training in Yemen was not a part of his background information. Since then, his file had been updated with his military record and his activities of interest. Red flagged reports were automatically generated and e-mail copies were sent to the FBI office in the city of origin, the FBI Special Regional Agent and the Homeland Security coordinator in DC.

When Ken Morrison turned on his computer after having his first cup of coffee, he saw the BOLO on Azlan Yardim. He ran an inquiry on the incident report database and found the missing person report Bonnie had filled out. The report listed Azlan's description and his home and work addresses. The comments section of the report said that the FBI should be contacted if there was any information on the whereabouts of this individual. Morrison understood that Azlan's connection to the liquor store would quickly lead to

Omar. Even if Omar and his boys were clean, he wouldn't want anyone looking in his direction. Morrison contemplated not warning Omar, but it might lead to the loss of his second source of income. He picked up the phone.

"This is Omar."

"The girlfriend filled out a missing persons report on Azlan. It says that he worked at the liquor store. You and your boys had better stay away from there."

"Damn! What else do they know about Azlan?"

"I don't know, but there is a request to contact the FBI with any information on his whereabouts."

"The FBI, maybe it's only a Visa problem," said Omar.

"Maybe, but why take the chance? By the way, I don't know what you guys are into. I'm guessing drugs or guns and I can go along with those vices. But, if I find out you're into any terrorist shit, I'll throw you to the wolves."

"Not to worry. Thanks for the call." Omar hung up. *Our friend is a man of principles. And maybe he's smarter than I thought.* Omar was involved in supplying both drugs and guns. But he wasn't involved in any terrorist acts; he just supported them.

Omar had Anwar make arrangements with Aalia and Hushni Salim to replace his men at the store. Omar didn't deal directly with Aalia and Hushni; they didn't even know his name. The store was to be taken care of by people who were clean. He had only used his men to work there to give them something to do until they were really needed. The store was not in Omar's name, neither was the apartment building. The last thing he needed was for the FBI to have eyes on his movements.

The red flagged missing person report found its way to the desk of agent Ron Sanders, a three-year man with the bureau. Agent Sanders had good bureau bloodlines; his father had been a Supervising Agent in LA before he retired and later expired. The old man had made a lot of friends in the bureau and young agent Sanders was being groomed for big things in the future. For now, he had to put in his time as a field agent and just not make any mistakes.

Sanders was twenty-six, and a graduate of Stanford School of Law. He was handsome, six foot one, one hundred ninety-five pounds, with brown hair and blue eyes. He was regularly called upon to interview female witnesses.

Agent Sanders had been asked to look into Azlan Yardim's movements up until his disappearance. Sanders found out from the FBI's Alien Monitoring System (AMS) that Yardim entered the country in 2003 on a student visa and he attended University of California Northridge briefly, then dropped out of sight.

Since Yardim entered the country, his FBI file had been updated twice. Once to add information that he had been an officer serving in Saddam's Royal Guard, and the second time to indicate that he had undergone training in Yemen. Now he turned up missing in South Florida. Agent Sanders thought this assignment was more busy work. But if Yardim was spotted here and picked up, questioning his ass might be interesting. There was only one place to start. He picked up the phone.

"Hello, I'd like to speak to Ms. Bonnie Rupp. Is she there?"

"Yeah, hold on."

After a minute or so, Bonnie picked up. "Hello, this is Bonnie Rupp."

"Ms. Rupp, my name is Agent Ronald Sanders with the Federal Bureau of Investigation. I'd like to talk to you about the missing person report you filed for Azlan Yardim."

"I don't know what more I can tell you; it's all in the report."

"Please, Ms. Rupp, it's important that I speak to you directly. I'm sure if I can have just a few minutes of your time, it might help find your friend."

"All right, but I'm working all day. It would help if you could come here. I'll have some free time at around two-fifteen. Does that work for you?"

"That's fine, I'll see you then."

"Goodbye."

Sanders hung up the phone and started his search in the FBI database for Bonnie Rupp. He assumed she'd be cooperative, but in case she wasn't, a little dirt might help her play ball. He searched the main data base, then local police files, but he found nothing usable.

She had taken out a restraining order on an ex-boyfriend eighteen months ago. Sanders was developing an image of Bonnie as a resilient woman who shook off a bad experience with one man and started seeing another. Or maybe she was just a good time girl. Sanders thought it would be best to reserve judgment on the young lady's character until the face to face. She could be just an innocent girl looking for her friend. In fact, if she knew her missing friend was a bad guy, she might not have gone to the police in the first place.

Agent Sanders entered the Three Flames Restaurant at exactly 2:15 pm. He walked to the hostess' desk and asked for Bonnie. The hostess started to pick up her phone, when she spotted Bonnie walking toward them. She was tall and well built, with a face that could sell cosmetics. She smiled as she approached Sanders and she extended her hand. He paused for a second and then took her hand. She didn't look like a woman who would be seen with a criminal. She looked more like someone you would see on the arm of an up-and-coming FBI agent.

"Agent Sanders, I'm Bonnie Rupp. I'm happy to meet you."

"Thank you for seeing me."

"We can talk in my office. Follow me." Bonnie led him to a small office in the back of the restaurant that doubled as a storage room. "Forgive the mess," she said as she sat behind the desk. Sanders eased into an unpadded chair facing the desk. "No problem. This should only take a few minutes. First of all, to be clear, you had a romantic relationship with Mr. Yardim. Is that correct?"

"Yes, that's right"

"How long have you known him?"

"About two and a half months. We met here at the restaurant."

"Where did Mr. Yardim work?"

"He told me that he owned a liquor store on Congress Avenue, but I think he just worked there."

"Did you have the occasion to meet any of Mr. Yardim's friends or associates?"

"No, he told me that he hadn't been in the area long

and he hadn't met many people. The friends we had were really my friends. He seemed to be a loner and he didn't talk at all about his friends or family."

"Ms. Rupp, the missing person report indicated that you had been contacted by one of Mr. Yardim's co-workers who told you that he left town, but you still went to the station and filled it out. Why?"

"It didn't make sense that Azlan would leave town without saying goodbye to me. We weren't planning to start a family or anything, but we were close. He wouldn't have just left without seeing me and explaining why he was going. Let me ask you a question, if I may."

"Okay, go ahead."

"Why is the FBI interested in a missing liquor store clerk?"

"There is a problem with Mr. Yardim's residency status. His visa expired several years ago."

"Wouldn't that be a problem for INS?"

"Yes, you're right. But it happens that Mr. Yardim has an extensive military service background from when he was in the Middle East. The combination of military service and expired visa raised a red flag in our office. That's why we're involved. We want to talk to Mr. Yardim."

Sanders questioned Bonnie for another fifteen minutes when, she began shortening her answers and looking at her watch.

"I know you're busy and I appreciate your taking the time to talk to me."

Bonnie smiled. "It's not a problem. Is there anything else?"

"No, that's all for now, but I may need to speak to you again. Also, if Mr. Yardim does contact you, I would appreciate it if you'd let me know." Sanders handed her his card.

Agent Sanders and Ms. Rupp said their goodbyes. Sanders left hoping that he would get the chance to see Bonnie Rupp again. And Bonnie hoped that she hadn't gotten Azlan into trouble.

Sanders spent the rest of the day interviewing Azlan Yardim's neighbors at his apartment building. He found out that Mr. Yardim kept to himself. He was quiet and had no pets. Occasionally, he had visitors, but recently there was only one blond lady who sometimes spent the night.

The building super let Sanders look at the apartment just as he had for the police officers that were also checking into this missing person. It was neat and clean with no mementos of its former occupant. The super said that Mr. Yardim left him a note saying that he was leaving the area. The note also contained enough money to pay the apartment rent up until the end of the month. Yardim was due a cleaning deposit that the super was holding for him.

Sanders was beginning to think there might be something to this sudden disappearance of Azlan Yardim. He might have been given an assignment in another city. Or he might have just completed an assignment here. Maybe he's been recalled to the Middle East. Sanders couldn't believe that Yardim voluntarily walked away from Ms. Rupp without a word. *"I wouldn't have done it,"* he said to himself, *"no way."*

CHAPTER SIXTEEN

Juan hadn't gotten much sleep before he had to go to work. He could hardly wait to see if his clue helped move the case forward. He thought about telling his father what he was doing but changed his mind. There was no chance that George would approve. And his disapproval might result in severe and painful repercussions.

Juan entered the conference room and noticed that something had changed. The board looked the same with his clues still there. He looked around and tried to remember the room as he left it sixteen hours ago. The chairs and table were the same. He looked at the walls and window, nothing. He looked up and then he saw it. A small security camera had been placed in the ceiling air vent. It would have gone unnoticed by anyone but Juan. *"They're on to me,'* he whispered. *'Oh Christ, I'm dead."*

He began working, cleaning up the conference room, not looking at the camera. When he finished, he left the room and completed the rest of his work, being careful not to do anything suspicious. He felt like he was holding his breath the whole shift and didn't relax until he was safely at home.

He went though his Criminology textbook looking for what constitutes hindering a criminal investigation. He tried to convince himself that he was helping, not hindering. He just had to play it cool and hope that nothing happened. He was sure that the security camera had just been placed in the room and wasn't there when he wrote on the board either time.

Juan went through the day trying to act as normal as possible. He went to class, but he couldn't remember what was discussed. At two o'clock, his usual bedtime, he tried to sleep but couldn't. He tossed and turned for an hour then got up. He turned on the TV, determined to just veg-out. The afternoon Court TV shows made him forget about his problems temporarily. After a while, he didn't care what he was watching.

The five o'clock news began with this story: "City detectives broke the Garrett triple murder case today. An anonymous tip led detectives to the chauffeur, who was using an alias and had a criminal history. The chauffeur, Brian Gaines aka Paul Winston, had a romantic relationship with the maid, who refused to go along with the robbery and was killed. Gaines and two criminal associates, David Patton and Gary Sawyer, admitted to committing the robbery and murders after being caught with the stolen items in their motel room. A search of Gaines' phone records revealed the relationship with the maid as well as the link to his criminal partners. This is the second major case solved by city detectives in less than a week."

Juan watched the entire newscast, hoping to get more information on the anonymous tip that helped solve the case, but there was nothing more. He looked at the clock. In five hours, he had to go back into work.

CHAPTER SEVENTEEN

Joey's aunt started missing him when she ran out of gin and had to switch to vodka. She hadn't seen him or his friend in three or four days. When she was down to her last cigarette, she had to go to the store herself. On the way to the corner store, she noticed Joey's car parked two doors down from the house. She knew Joey never walked anywhere, so after getting her carton of cigarettes and 1.75 liters of gin, she called the police. She convinced the officer that she couldn't make it down to the station, so they came to her and she filed missing person reports for Joey Adams and Edward Donovan.

The city had averaged less than one missing person a month for the past five years, so three in a week raised some eyebrows at the station. Edward Donovan and his known associate, Joey Adams, were being sought in connection with a stolen vehicle. Mac Archer, the officer in charge of the case, was notified that his prime suspect was now a missing person. He remembered the unsolicited assist he was getting on the case and he called detective Morrison.

"Ken, Mac here. Did you get anywhere with the Donovan list of known associates I sent you a couple of days ago?"

"No, sorry, something came up and I haven't got around to it."

"Well one of the names on the list, Joey Adams, just became a missing person along with our boy Eddie Donovan. I wanted to let you know, if you do ever get around to it, you'll be working on two cases at once."

"I don't know, it could be one case if the boys stole the car, felt bad and took off for parts unknown," said Morrison. "With my current case load, I don't think I'll be looking into the mysterious case of the stolen and returned car after all."

"Sorry to hear that, I thought I was going to get some free help here."

"Maybe next time. Take it easy."

Morrison hung up and dialed Omar's number.

"This is Omar."

"Omar, missing person reports were just filed for the two guys I fingered for you."

"They had to be eliminated. What did you expect?"

"I expected you to convince them to return your property, put the fear of God in them and let them go."

"They saw too much, they knew too much. They killed one of my men and they knew that I covered it up. Sooner or later, they'd come back to haunt me. What does it matter anyway? Who cares about two ex-cons?"

"Too much blood is being spilled. The cost of my cooperation just doubled."

There was a moment of silence, and then Omar said, "That's kind of expensive for someone who doesn't get his hands dirty."

"That's the way it is. Either it's a deal or I walk away."

"Okay, okay, no problem," said Omar.

"And from now on, I don't want to be involved with any more wet work. Understood?"

"Sure, sure, understood."

Omar hung up the phone and wondered how much heat would result from a detective who went missing.

CHAPTER EIGHTEEN

Juan went to work expecting to clean up after another celebration in the detective squad conference room. He was right; the place was a mess. The trash cans were filled with dirty paper plates and cups, and there was confetti and streamers all over the floor. He glanced at the whiteboard and saw that the details of a new case covered it. He strained to keep himself from studying the new case. He knew it was a trap. The security camera was still there. He wasn't going to do anything to implicate himself. He went about his work quickly, he finished and left.

He knew there were very few civilians who had access to the building and only a handful that could get in the second floor conference room. *"Why did they go to the expense of a security camera when all they had to do was interview maybe five people at most? They probably didn't want to stop the person leaving the tips; they just wanted to find out who it was."* Regardless, Juan was done. No more cases, no more tips, no more trouble.

Agent Sanders started his day with an early morning jog in the park near his condo. He did three miles every other day. If he didn't jog, he went to the gym on the first floor of his building and worked out for an hour. He'd shower, shave and make it to the office by eight thirty.

He planned to spend the morning at Azlan Yardim's

place of business, the liquor store. The store didn't open until 10:00 am, so agent Sanders reviewed the agency on-line update memos and briefs.

At 10:08 am, agent Sanders pulled up at the liquor store and parked in one of the seven spaces allotted for it. He hadn't spent much time in this part of the city, so he looked up the crime statistics for the area before he left the office. The area had its share of break-ins and car thefts. He made note of the security camera in the strip mall across the street and he went in the store. He introduced himself to the owners, Aalia and Hushni Salim.

"I'm looking for an employee of yours, Azlan Yardim," he said.

"Yes, Azlan, a good man, a very good man. We're sorry he left us. Hard worker, good man."

"How long did he work for you?"

"He worked here for thirteen months. Always on time, dependable, never any trouble." The Salims had been well coached. Their answers appeared to be honest and spontaneous.

"You called Azlan's girlfriend and told her that he said he was leaving town. Is that right?"

"Yes, Azlan came in to pick up his pay. He said that he was leaving the area, something about trouble at home with his family."

"When was his last day at work?"

"That was last Friday night, 10:00 pm to 6:00 am Saturday morning shift."

"Did he leave a forwarding address or contact number?"

"No, we told all this to the police officers who came by two days ago."

"Just trying to be thorough." The questioning continued for another ten minutes, but the Salims had nothing more to add. Agent Sanders thanked them for their cooperation, gave them his card and left.

He walked across the street to the strip mall security office and introduced himself. Sanders found out that he was not the only one interested in the security footage covering Azlan's last shift. The mall guard didn't remember the name of the cop who asked about the tape, but he did give Sanders a description of him. Sanders also got a copy of the tapes covering Friday and Saturday of the previous week.

Back at the office, Sanders went through his hard copy mail and his e-mail. Then, after he filled his supervisor in on his progress, Sanders set up the VCR and settled in his chair to review the tapes. The mall security camera was set up to scan the parking lot and not the liquor store across the street, but the store was visible in the background. The store's distance from the camera was a problem, but the tape could be used to identify a person's gender and approximate their height and weight.

At 9:50 pm on Friday, he saw someone fitting Azlan Yardim's description entering the store, and then there was a procession of people entering and leaving the store up until midnight. There was no activity until 1:35 am. An old Pontiac Firebird parked and a man with a slight build went in the store. A minute later another man exited the car and ran into the store. Eight minutes later both men left the store and pulled off. There was no activity until 7:00 am when a heavyset man hesitated at the doorway, then entered the store. An hour later, the heavy man locked the store and drove away. Forty minutes later heavy man returned, unlocked and entered the store. There was no activity until 10:20 am, then what appeared to be normal store traffic started up.

At 1:10 pm a man in a suit entered the store. The same man left the store twenty minutes later and stood in the parking lot looking around. After a minute, he walked across the street towards the camera in the strip mall. As he approached, he could be seen clearly. He stayed in the mall for forty minutes and then left and went back to his car across the street and drove off. The tape continued for eight more hours, showing nothing of interest.

Agent Sanders watched the tape twice. The second time, he jotted down notes on the events and their sequence. He also made a still photograph of the man in the suit who told the mall guard that he was a policeman. Sanders recognized a robbery when he saw one; there was no doubt in his mind that the liquor store had been hit early Saturday morning. However, the police response was not normal. A plain-clothes cop showed up the afternoon after the crime. It didn't make sense. He made a database inquiry for reported robberies in the city on Saturday. A gas station holdup and a convenience store robbery were the only two incidents reported on that date.

"If the store was hit, why wasn't the robbery reported?" he asked himself. *"But a cop did show up the next day, so it was reported to someone."* He made another database inquiry and found that a 1992 Pontiac Firebird had been reported stolen on that date. He replayed the tape in his head, noting the significant activities shown and he realized that something was missing. The man fitting Azlan's description never left the store.

CHAPTER NINETEEN

Omar was annoyed that he could no longer use the liquor store as a front for his other businesses. It had the advantage of having people passing through those doors all day without raising any suspicions. Even though he only went there once a week, it was very convenient. Now drops had to be made elsewhere.

Omar's principal businesses were heroine and gun sales. He had established his drug connections when he was in the fighting in Afghanistan. Omar's father had been in the army and was able to provide some in-roads for his son. As it turns out, Omar was a good soldier and an even better leader. He rose in the ranks and at the age of 23, he commanded over a hundred men.

In addition to fighting the war, Omar's mission was to help protect the drug trade with the west. He was able to amass a small fortune from the drug trade without jeopardizing his position in the military. With his power as a military commander, and his contacts with the smugglers and the farmers, Omar became a very important man.

He became important enough to be a prime target for the Russians and envious sub-commanders on his own side. He was aware of the circumstances and he was careful to surround himself with loyal men.

He fought for years and he didn't see anything change. The drug trade continued, he lost more and more men and the fighting went on and on. He grew more and more discouraged.

One day, without telling anyone, he picked ten trusted men to replace a group of smugglers carrying raw heroin west. Omar, his men, and his money worked their way across the continent. They lived in Saudi Arabia for a time and then it was just a matter of money to get to South America and later, North America. Of the eleven men who started the journey, three made it to the end, Omar, Hassan and Anwar. The others wanted to stay behind and make lives for themselves in Europe and South America. Omar allowed it and he used those comrades to set up his drug and gun pipelines.

Omar established himself in South Florida and was able to make a place for others who were able to enter the country. With his military and financial contacts, Omar had guns smuggled into the country. He supplied militia groups in the mid-west, which appeared to be growing. With his drug connections, he supplied heroin by the kilo to gangs on the east coast.

Within five years, Omar had thirteen men working for him, some of them distant relatives. All of them were ex-military. Most had legitimate day jobs, also working for Omar. They worked in his appliance store or his auto body shop or his supermarket. Nothing was in Omar's name, but everything was under his control.

He was careful not to get directly involved in any operation. Dealing with the thieves, Eddie and Joey, was an exception. Omar had to make sure he recovered the document that was stolen. He had agreed to support an operation by passing a document to contacts from Canada who were expected to arrive soon. Passing the document as promised was a matter of life or death, Omar's own life or death.

Omar was a rich man, but he didn't live a life of luxury. He was comfortable, but nothing more. The goal of Omar's organization was to undermine the country. Selling guns to the crazy whites of the mid-west and selling poison to the blacks and browns on the east coast served his purpose well. Occasionally one of Omar's men would make contact with a cell or group of individuals who needed financial support. Omar would provide the required support without asking for any details of the group's plans. Omar's men were under strict orders not to establish any permanent connection with any terrorist group. They were to be kept at arm's length.

Omar was loyal to his homeland, but his family and his people here came first. He had worked hard to get where he was and he wanted to protect his people and himself. He heard the politicians tell the world how great the United States was, and how everyone was free and he saw the prejudice and the injustice. He experienced the discrimination against the Muslims. And he saw discrimination against the blacks and the browns. He also saw how the women dressed and acted and how they emasculated their men. He knew the country was going straight to hell. So why not help it along.

Anwar had been working on a new gun deal. The mid-west militias became more and more interested in heavy weapons that were harder to get, and less interested in the handguns that Omar was selling. The drug gang used and needed handguns for their day-to-day business and Omar's people had no problem getting them at a good price. It seemed like a perfect fit. Sell both guns and drugs to the gangs. Anwar wondered why it hadn't been thought of before.

When the idea was brought to Omar, he thought about it for a minute and said, "Don't the gangs already have gun suppliers?"

"I'm sure they do, but we could undercut their price," Anwar countered.

"We would be taking over someone's business and making a new enemy. Before we do this, we first need to know a few things."

"What would that be?"

"What's the profit potential? Who's the competition? What are their strengths and weaknesses? Will they fight to keep their customers? This may turn out to be a good idea, but first do a little research."

"Okay, I'll call our east coast friends and ask a few questions. It never hurts to ask."

"Fine," said Omar as he got up and adjusted the office air conditioner. Omar had moved his office to his auto body shop in Port St. Lucie. The office was noisy and dirty and a bad commute. Fortunately, he only used it a few hours a week. He spent most of his time expanding his legitimate businesses.

He thought about Anwar's idea; it was a good one, but it had a drawback that concerned him. It would mean expanding his operation, bringing in more men. Staying under the radar was difficult enough with the people he already had.

The problems with Azlan and his trouble-making girlfriend had shown Omar that single men should not be a part of his group. He thought to himself for a minute, counting on his fingers. He had five men working for him who were not married. He decided that he would marry them off, and not to any blond, air-headed American girl. He would find good girls with good values who knew their place.

CHAPTER TWENTY

Juan had spent the last two days being perfect. He did absolutely nothing wrong. He studied for class, did his homework, cleaned his room, and volunteered to run errands. He was a model citizen. After a while, he began to relax; he felt he was in the clear. On campus at school, he thought he was being watched, but he quickly dismissed the idea.

He went to work believing everything was fine. He worked his way through the restrooms and the office areas. When he entered the conference room, he found two detectives sitting at the table. One was tall and athletic looking, about thirty years old, with a thin face and a crooked smile. He was wearing a brown suit, a yellow shirt, with his tie undone. The other man was shorter, older and heavier, with a square jaw and a know-it-all grin. He had on a blue shirt and black slacks.

Brown suit said, "Hello Juan, I'm Detective Dave Littlefield and this is my partner, Detective Don Collins. How are you doing?"

"Fine, sir, I didn't mean to disturb you; I'll come back later to clean up."

"No, no, Son. We're here to see you."

"You want to see me?" Juan's heart stopped. "Why do you want to see me?"

"You know, Juan. Come on; let's be honest with each other. You know what you did; you might as well admit it."

"I don't know what you're talking about."

"Of course you do, but let me refresh your memory. You interfered with a police investigation, in fact, two police investigations. Remember the doctor's wife's murder and the triple homicide cases?"

Juan paused for a second, "Didn't you guys solve those cases?"

The detectives looked at each other, and detective Littlefield said, "Maybe we should bring your parents in and we'll all sit down and talk."

Juan said, "That's not a good idea."

"Why not?"

"First of all, my father will give me hell. My mother, on the other hand, will come at you two like a freight train. She'll say that you violated my rights by talking to me without her permission. Then she'll go to the chief of detectives and charge you with harassing a minor. And when the chief of detectives finds out that the bottom line is that I helped you solve two cases, he'll question your competence for detective work and your sanity for raising a stink in the first place. Should I go on?"

The detectives looked at each other again; this time they broke out laughing. "Okay, you got us, Juan. Let's talk off the record."

"Off the record?"

"Yeah. How about it?"

Juan said, "Okay, first turn off the security camera."

Littlefield and Collins took Juan to a storage room that he didn't have access to and showed him the security camera set up. Collins pushed the off button on the recording device. They walked to Collins' desk and sat down around it.

"How'd you do it?" Collins asked.

"I just looked at the clues and came up with alternate theories."

"Nobody helped you or told you about the case?" Littlefield asked.

"No, I just studied the facts and clues you guys put together. But don't worry; I'll never do it again.

The detectives looked at each other, this time no smiles or laughter. "Your clues helped us, Juan. Maybe you just had a couple of lucky guesses, maybe not. Now that we know what you've been doing, we can work together to see whether or not it was just luck."

Collins leaned toward Juan, lowering his voice, "Obviously, it wouldn't look good for us if people knew that we were being helped by a seventeen year old. So let's keep this just between us, okay?"

"That's fine with me." Juan shook both their hands, relieved that he could stop looking over his shoulder and imagining the worst.

"We'll have the security camera removed from the conference room, but from now on, don't leave your clues on the whiteboard. Put them on a piece of paper and leave them on one of our desks."

"Deal!" said Juan with big smile.

CHAPTER TWENTY ONE

Agent Sanders showed the still photograph to an officer from city's Internal Affairs Department. The officer recognized Detective Ken Morrison and provided some background information on him. Internal Affairs had looked at Morrison in the past, but was never able to tie him to anything serious.

Back at the Flagler Drive office, Sanders scheduled a meeting to update his supervisor. He also got printouts of Morrison's phone records for the last three months. The phone records had Morrison making several calls to a cell phone. There was no way of finding out whom he was calling on that phone. His other calls were more helpful. There were several calls between Morrison and Officer Mac Archer who worked in Auto Thefts. Sanders had an idea. He picked up his phone.

"This is Mac."

"Officer Archer, my name is Ron Sanders, in the FBI area office. We're calling around looking for any information on a gang that targets older cars for specific parts. Cars are not stolen, just broken into for original parts. Since the parts are sold across state lines, the FBI is involved. Has anything come across your desk that looks like it might fit my case?"

"Yeah, a week ago, we caught a strange one. A car was broken into and the ignition wires were stripped; we thought it was stolen and returned. It could have just been broken into and vandalized."

"That sounds close enough. Did you find out

anything?"

"The car had blood stains left in it and it was towed to police impound and examined. There was nothing missing from the car. We found a set of fingerprints belonging to a small time criminal named Eddie Donovan."

"Could you send me a copy of everything you've got on this one?"

"Sure, you know, you're not the first guy to ask about this car. One of our detectives was looking into this case for a short while, but he got busy with other work."

"Who was that?"

"Guy by the name of Ken Morrison. Look him up, maybe he can add something."

"Thanks, I appreciate the help. By the way, what was the make of the car?"

"It was a 1992 Pontiac Firebird."

"Thanks again." Sanders hung up and walked down the hall to the office of Special Agent Eric Lacey, Sanders' immediate supervisor. He sat down in the guest chair opposite Lacey's desk and waited quietly until his supervisor finished his make the subordinate wait ritual. Then Lacey looked up and nodded, and said, "So, what have you got?"

"I traced Yardim to the liquor store, and I found a working security camera in a strip mall across the street. The security footage showed Yardim entering the store for his shift on the nineteenth, Friday evening. It looks like the liquor store was hit. Then a heavyset guy shows up at 7:00 am, enters the store. Heavy is in the store for about an hour, then he locks the store and leaves. Heavy shows up forty-five minutes later and enters the store. At 10:00 am, it looks like regular store traffic starts up. A Detective Ken Morrison shows up at 1:10 pm, enters the store and stays inside for about an hour. Morrison comes out, looks around and crosses the street and goes in the strip mall. He leaves the mall after about thirty minutes and gets in his car and drives off. It looks like Morrison was called to find the robbers quietly."

"Why not call the regular cops?"

"Maybe Azlan Yardim got hurt or dead and they didn't want him found at the store; or maybe something like jewels or drugs were taken that couldn't be reported stolen."

"So you think this heavy set gentleman is trying to solve the case quietly?" Lacey was trying to appear interested.

"The heavy man was the first one on the scene after the robbery. He most likely made the call to Morrison. He's the key to what's going on. He must have been the one who decided to cover up the robbery."

"The only thing that should concern us is the missing alien. Everything else belongs to the locals," said Lacey.

"There's a lot going on here. If I follow it all, something else will turn up on our plate. At the very least, we'll get an award from the city for helping clean up its streets."

"Okay, keep working, but don't share anything with the locals unless absolutely necessary."

"Yes, Sir." Sanders got up and went back to his desk. This meeting had gone better than he expected. Lacey had been with the bureau for twenty-eight years. He was retired in place and he wasn't looking to rock the boat. Two more years and he would be actually retired.

Sanders called his contact in the Internal Affairs Department.

"It looks like your boy Morrison might be involved in one of our cases dealing with the disappearance of an illegal alien."

"What have you got that you can share?"

"Not much yet. But I can say that it looks like Detective Morrison has more than one employer," said Sanders.

"It wouldn't look good if our detective was picked up by the FBI. We need to be part of this investigation."

"Precisely why I called. We're about to put a tail on Morrison and a tap on his phones, but I think I can convince my boss to let Internal Affairs do it. That's if you guys share everything you find."

"That sounds good to me as long as sharing goes both ways."

"Let me run it by my boss and I'll call you later to work out the details." Sanders hung up. He had no intention of running the idea of working with IA by his boss. He was just going to do it. He figured that Morrison would lead Internal Affairs right to Eddie Donovan and his partner and then to whomever was paying to find them.

Sanders did his usual afternoon Incident Report Data Base search and found a missing persons report for one Edward Donovan. Sanders expanded his search and found that both Eddie Donovan and Joey Adams had been reported missing by Estelle Adams. Sanders waited for an hour and then he called IA and told them it was okay to go ahead and tail Morrison.

CHAPTER TWENTY-TWO

Juan was having a good day. Now that he was not in any trouble and actually working with the detectives, life was beautiful. He was tempted to tell George what he was doing, but he decided not to until he actually proved to be useful. He rushed through his work in order to spend more time in the conference room studying the facts and clues of the latest high profile case. When he got there, he found that things were back to normal. There were no detectives and no surveillance camera.

The new case was a series of three home invasion robberies, each two weeks apart. So far, one person had been home during the second robbery and she, a woman 73 years old, had been strangled to death. The robbers had forced their way into each residence by breaking windows or sliding glass doors. All the houses were upscale, on several acres of land, and none of the neighbors were close enough to hear anything. Nothing big was taken, just cash and jewelry and laptop computers.

The detectives were trying to find a connection between the victims. There didn't appear to be any. They didn't frequent the same stores or belong to the same clubs and the families weren't of the same age group. The detectives looked for servicemen and repairmen who might have recently been at the houses.

Juan studied the crime scene pictures and the notes on the board and the descriptions of the victims and the missing items. He decided that he had too much information. The other cases he looked at were single incidents; this one with three crimes was overwhelming. He stepped back and looked around the room. The information laid out was jumbled. In some places, the facts were presented as if it was one case, in other places; it looked like three separate cases. The information needed to be better organized.

He wondered how well it would go over with the detectives if he left a note saying "organize your information better." Juan shrugged his shoulders and left the room.

Juan sat down at Detective Collins' desk and wrote a note. He shook his head, folded the note and left it in the center of the desk. He finished his shift in a lot worst mood than when he started it, and he went home.

Collins found the note first thing the next morning. He read it.

I studied the information in the conference room. I couldn't figure it out from the way it's laid out. It needs to be laid out like three separate cases side by side. Maybe then something might jump out at me. All I could get from what I saw was that the bad guys take two weeks to identify and learn about the victims. Then they pull the job and move on. To my way of thinking, two weeks isn't long enough to learn about the habits and movements of a target. I think it's an inside job. Actually, I think it's three inside jobs. The bad guys take two weeks to learn about the target and talk to someone on the inside who knows about the target. I know you're pissed at me for telling you how to organize your facts, so it's been nice working with you.

Juan

Collins sat at his desk motionless, staring at the note.

"Morning, Don, what's up?" said Littlefield.

Collins tossed the note to his partner at the adjacent desk. "Take a look at that."

"That little punk, where does he get the nerve to tell us how to ..."

"Calm down and read the whole note. I think that the kid is on to something. It's been bothering me how the robbers could know everything they need to know to do these jobs in two weeks. They get next to someone who has the information they need. Information like: When do they go out? Do they always turn on the security system? Are they loaded? Stuff like that."

"Okay I see what you're saying." Littlefield was slowly coming on board.

"And the insider doesn't need to be inside. A mailman, pool man or a gardener or somebody like that could supplement what the bad guy learns in his two weeks in the area. It makes sense."

"What do you want to do now?"

"How about we go in the conference room and arrange things to look like three cases, side by side?"

"Sounds like a good idea. If we hurry, we can have it ready for the boss when he comes in tonight," joked Littlefield.

CHAPTER TWENTY-THREE

For Omar, things were getting back to normal. He arranged to have the new office fixed up and cleaned. He was still weighing the idea of selling guns to his drug customers. Anwar had done his research and all Omar's questions had been answered. Now he knew who the opposition was and what the costs would be for horning in on their business.

He had seen enough bloodshed to last him for a while. The loss of Azlan affected him and he knew it. It would disappoint Anwar if his idea was rejected, but the cost was too high. Omar decided that it would be a mistake to expand his operation. Anwar had to be told in a way that showed he was respected and his ideas were valued. He put his Anwar problem aside for the moment.

The five unmarried men that worked for Omar filed into his office. Omar had called each of them to attend a short meeting. He gave them the good news that each of them would soon be married.

"I don't know why your families haven't already arranged things for you. Each of you is to let your families know that steps are to be taken to find suitable mates from our community. No outsiders are to be considered. If any of you have relationships with western women, end those relationships now."

He could see the surprise in the faces of his men. One of them, Muneer, had a look that wasn't surprise; it was defiance. Omar leveled his gaze at Muneer and said, "If you don't want to follow my orders, you are free to leave my employ."

Muneer lowered his eyes. Finding another job would be difficult. Although Muneer and the others weren't illegal, a new employer's background check wouldn't be welcomed. And even though Omar said they could leave, they were sure that there would be repercussions. There weren't any questions, and the meeting ended with everyone in agreement. The husbands to be went back to work.

Alone in his office, Omar again struggled with how he should deal with Anwar. Anwar was a soldier and a good one. He would follow orders, no questions asked, and Omar had been grooming him to be his replacement. Anwar had shown initiative that should be rewarded, not dismissed. He called Anwar and told him to come to the office. Twenty minutes later, Anwar knocked and came in. "Have you considered my idea to increase gun sales?"

"Yes, it's a good idea, but we'll have to put it aside for now. There's something more important I want you to do."

Anwar grinded his teeth, trying to hide his disappointment, "What is it you want me to do?"

"I want you to organize and plan a mission. These soldiers of ours need to be given a job to do to remind them of who they are and what they can do. Providing security for gun and drug shipments isn't enough to feed their pride. They need to train, plan for and practice an operation just like our brothers are doing back home."

"You want us to mount an attack here?" Anwar asked.

"An assault, not an attack. You're going to commit a robbery. You will take a team of men and rob a bank or jewelry store, whatever you decide. I want the haul to be as large as possible."

"Are you really serious about this?"

"Absolutely. I want you to pick eight men and get them in shape. I also want you to pick four targets in different areas of the city. Develop plans to rob each target. I don't know how much time you have to get ready, so you should start immediately."

"I don't understand. Do we have a time-table?"

Omar smiled. "I know this sounds crazy, but listen. Imagine if someone had planned and executed a robbery in New York on September eleventh. They could have walked away and no one would have paid any attention to them. All the cops in the city were fully engaged elsewhere. If we had known what was going to happen, we could have walked into any bank or jewelry store unopposed."

"Do you know when another 9/11 is going to happen?"

"Not yet, but soon. We have a lot of work to do to get ready."

CHAPTER TWENTY-FOUR

When Juan showed up for work and went to the second floor, Collins and Littlefield were there waiting for him. They smiled when they saw him. "We've been waiting for you. Your idea about this being an inside job was a good one." Collins made the four-fingered quotes gesture when he said 'inside job'.

"Yeah kid, we laid out the facts of the case the way you said." Littlefield added.

"We did a little more than just format things differently. We were able to see that each family had a few things in common. Each used a lawn service, each had groceries delivered, and they all ate out on a regular basis, etc. After eliminating a few common items, we zeroed in on the lawn service. Each family used a different lawn service, but those services hire and fire people all the time. We got ahold of the owners and found out that each employed the same man for a short time before each of the break-ins. The guy's name is Vincent Frizzano and he's got a record for Breaking and Entering and he's out on parole."

"We've got a team sitting on him right now, waiting for him to hook up with his playmates and pull another job. Once we get them all together, we'll take them down," Littlefield said colorfully for Juan's benefit.

"It would be nice to catch them in the act. We can toss his place anytime we want and we're getting a tap on his phone. It's just a matter of time before we get them. Good work, kid."

"I thought I blew it," said Juan.

"No way kid, you're a natural."

"I don't know about that. But if you think I'm helping, maybe you can arrange for me to be compensated for my work."

The smile on Collins' face disappeared. "I don't know, we're still doing this under the table."

"Could it be time to go public?" Juan asked.

"Maybe we should get a few more cases under our belts first. I'll tell you what I can do. We have a few bucks set aside in the squad for Confidential Informants. We could divert some money your way. How does fifty bucks a week sound?"

"Fifty bucks whether I work on a case or not. That sounds good to me."

"Okay, but our deal is that you tell nobody about this. You don't tell your family or friends what you're doing."

"That's the deal," said Juan, thrilled with the arrangement.

Juan wasn't the only one thrilled with the arrangement. Collins and Littlefield's stars were rising. No one else in the department had closed back-to-back cases in such short order. Fifty bucks a week was a small enough price to pay for super stardom. Everyone from the other detectives to the people that really mattered was impressed. Collins would be looking for a bump to first grade if they solved another case or two.

When a couple of detectives cornered Littlefield in the locker room and tried to pump him for the secret to his new found success, he told them that he and Collins had got a new

CI who turned out to be a gold mine. That admission turned out to be a mistake. The other guys in the squad began to watch them closely, hoping to find out who their new CI was.

CHAPTER TWENTY FIVE

Sanders was sure that putting a tail on Detective Morrison wouldn't produce anything, but he hoped Morrison would spot the tail and do something stupid. IA reported that Morrison was acting like a model citizen.

"The guy does his job and goes home with a regular stop at a bar near his place. Either he's clean or he's very careful. My money's on careful."

"I'm sure he's dirty. It might take a while to prove it," said Sanders. "If you need to move on with something else, let me know. We'll take over."

"No, that's all right, we'll hang in a little longer."

Sanders knew he had nowhere else to go. Having Morrison on the strip mall's security tape was nothing; a crime hadn't even been reported. He searched the FBI database for anything that might be related to a sighting of Azlan Yardim, nothing. The only thing that caught his eye was a report that came in about campers in Wetlands State Park discovering two bodies. The local authorities were on the scene. The bodies belonged to two white men with multiple gunshots to the back of their heads. Sanders had to wait for the bodies to be identified, but he knew they were Eddie Donovan and Joey Adams.

Now Sanders had a crime, but unless there was some evidence at the scene, he couldn't tie Morrison to it. The crime wasn't under the jurisdiction of the FBI, and it never would be unless it could be tied to Azlan. Sanders locked his desk and told the secretary that he was on his way to a crime scene in Wetlands State Park.

It was a thirty-five mile trip, but it seemed a lot longer. With mid-day traffic, it took him a little under an hour to get there. The local police department and park rangers were well represented. They were stepping all over each other destroying the crime scene. There was no hope of getting the shoe prints or tire prints of the killer. The bodies were a mess. Both were shot in the back of the head with large facial exit wounds. One was also shot in the knee. It didn't look like either of the dead men fought back. That indicated that the victims were under control and there was probably more than one killer.

After the medical examiner was finished with his work, the local police went though the victims' belongings. It wasn't a robbery; both victims had cash on them and their IDs. The victims were identified as Edward Donovan and Joey Adams. According to his driver's license Adams' address was 738 Westgate Avenue. Sanders was not there in any official capacity, so he thanked the locals for their cooperation and left.

Sanders wanted to talk to the aunt before she was informed of Joey's demise and got too emotional to be questioned. He needed to use the car's GPS to get to Westgate Avenue. He rang the bell, and after a few minutes, an old lady appeared at the door. "Mrs. Adams?"

"It's Ms. Adams," said the old lady.

"Ms. Adams, my name is Agent Ronald Sanders of the FBI and I'm looking for your nephew Joseph. Is he here?"

"No, he's been gone for almost a week now. I put in a missing person on him. Nobody found him yet. They ain't told me if they did."

"Tell me, did anyone come to the house looking for Joey before he disappeared? Possibly, this man." Sanders showed her the still picture of Morrison taken from the mall security tape.

"Yeah, he was here, an insurance guy I think. Yeah, that's him."

"Good, that will help. One more thing, what kind of car does Joey drive?"

"That one right there up the street." She pointed at a green Camaro parked two doors away.

"Do you have the key?"

"Yeah, he keeps an extra one in the house. I'll get it for you."

With the key, Sanders opened the car and started searching through the glove compartment. There was nothing important in the car, but he did notice the faint smell of bleach. Sanders returned the key to Ms. Adams. "I'm sorry, but it looks like we'll have to come back and take the car and examine it."

"That's no problem for me, I don't drive anyway."

"Thank you for all your help. Goodbye."

To Sanders, bleach in the car meant someone was trying to clean up some bloodstains. He thought that if bloodstains could be found in Joey's car and they matched the stains found in the stolen car left at the hospital, he could link Joey and Eddie to the liquor store. The tape linked Morrison to the liquor store and now Auntie Adams linked Morrison to Joey. Sanders had something, but he didn't know exactly what."

Sanders put in a call to Internal Affairs and suggested there was a connection between Morrison and the double homicide in Wetlands State Park. He told them that one of the victims' car might have clues supporting that theory, and that a thorough examination of the car would be a good idea.

CHAPTER TWENTY-SIX

It was 5:00 pm when George woke his son from a sound sleep. "Juan, get up, something's happened and we have to go."

"Is it time for work already?"

"No, but we have to go."

"Go where, what's wrong?"

"Your sister's been in an accident. We have to go to her now."

Juan got up and sat on the side of his bed and tried to clear his head. He could hear his mother crying in the next room and he hurried to put on his clothes. He rushed out of his bedroom and saw his mother, father and little sister, Annette, all in tears waiting for him in the hallway.

"What's going on?" Juan shouted.

"Let's get in the car," said George.

"Will someone please tell me what's going on?"

Juan's mother, Marie, fought back her tears and said, "Rose was really hurt; someone held her up and stole her car. We need to go to the hospital now."

It was a fifty-minute ride to the hospital in Fort Lauderdale. Juan continued to ask questions most of the way until George had reached his limit and told him to shut up. Everyone was thinking the worst. Marie was able to reach Steve, Rose's husband, on the cell phone, but the reception was terrible. Steve tried his best to dodge Marie's questions, but finally had to tell her that Rose had been shot and she was being operated on. Marie screamed and George nearly drove the car into the railing. Juan took the phone and got as much information as he could while he tried to calm his mother. The ride seemed to take forever, only Annette appeared to be in control of her emotions.

They parked at the Emergency entrance and ran to the nurse's station and were directed to the Surgical Unit. They saw Steve in the hall talking to a policeman. Marie ran to Steve screaming, "You took my baby from me and see what's happened. I hate you. I hate you."

George caught up to Marie and pulled her away from Steve and asked. "What's happening, Son? How is she?"

"I don't know, they haven't told me anything. Oh God! I don't know."

George put his arms around Steve and held him while he broke down and cried. Marie pulled herself together and stepped inside George and held Steve and said, "I'm sorry, I'm sorry."

Juan walked over to the policeman. "Did they catch the guy yet?"

"No, not yet, but the description of the car has been sent out to all patrols."

"Is there a suspect description out there as well?"

"No, not yet. We have to wait until we can talk to the victim."

Juan felt his gut tighten when he heard Rose being referred to as a victim. "Do you know how many shots were fired or how many times she was hit?"

"There were multiple shots fired. She didn't want to give up the car. The Emergency Services guys didn't say if she was hit more than once."

Juan walked back to where the family was waiting and he sat down. He had no more questions to ask and he had all the answers he could handle at the moment. He didn't want to play policeman any more, now was the time to be the little brother. He saw Marie's lips moving and he joined her in prayer. Time stood still while they waited. Juan counted the people walking by the waiting area, and then he started on the little holes in the ceiling tiles.

The surgeon came out of the operating room an hour later. He apologized and said that his team had done everything they could, but the wound was too severe and she had lost too much blood. Marie collapsed and George caught her before she hit the floor; Annette began to howl. The men stayed in control, but Steve looked like he was in shock. The doctor was more concerned about him than he was about Marie.

No one spoke on the ride home. Marie and Annette held each other and wept all the way. It was 10:24 pm when they made it home. George put Marie to bed and Annette and Juan went to their rooms. George sat in his chair and looked around the room. His gaze stopped on the family portrait on the mantelpiece. *"I still have two children,"* he said to himself as if he was looking for a reason to go on with his life. He sat quietly for ten minutes, then he got up.

"Juan, time for work."

Juan heard him, but he wasn't sure he believed him. Juan came out of his room and asked, "Are you serious?"

"You can stay here and deal with your pain and I'll understand. For me, I have to go in. I won't be able to sleep anyway, and I don't want to be left alone with my thoughts."

Juan didn't say anything; he got his lunch bag and went to the car.

CHAPTER TWENTY-SEVEN

"Shit!" said Morrison when he read the bulletin that reported a double homicide in Wetlands State Park. He hoped the bodies would never be found. The bulletin didn't contain any details of the crime, but the bodies had been identified. He wanted to call Omar and tell him about the incompetents he had working for him. He decided to calm down and inform Omar of what was going on and get another payday. He dialed the phone number.

"This is Omar."

"The cops found two bodies in the park."

"We expected them to be found eventually."

"Eventually maybe, but not after ten days. Do your guys know what they're doing?"

"What's the problem?"

"I don't know yet, but if one mistake has been made, many others could be out there waiting to bite us in the ass. Talk to your guys; find out if they did anything else stupid. I'll find out how the investigation is coming along."

"Okay, keep in touch." Omar hung up and leaned back in his chair. After a few moments, he called Hassan. "Hassan, I just got a call from our friend with the police. The bodies have been found."

"We dumped them like the garbage that they were. We didn't try to hide them. And we left no clues that would lead them to us."

"Our policeman friend is worried. He'll follow the investigation and let us know what's going on."

"Do we care?"

"We do if the investigation leads back to us. But, as I see it right now, our only loose end is our connection to our policeman friend."

"Do you want me to take care of him?"

"No, he is a valuable resource. He's our early warning system. If later on he proves to be a liability, we'll deal with him. I just want you to know, that he is not untouchable."

At 11:00 pm, when Juan entered the squad room almost in tears, Collins was waiting for him. "What's wrong, kid?"

"My sister was killed today."

"What happened?"

"She was car-jacked and shot on her way home from work."

"Did they catch the guy?"

"No, not yet. They don't even have a description." Juan was ready to fall apart; tears were streaming down his cheeks. "I don't know what to do."

"There's nothing you can do, kid. Just try to be strong for your family and don't give them anything else to worry about. What are you doing coming to work? Shouldn't you be home with your family?"

"My mother's resting and my father thought we should

stay busy."

"Okay, your dad knows best. Try to take it easy."

"Did you come here tonight to see me?"

"Yes, I wanted to talk about the home invasion case and to give you this." Collins had a package in his hand.

"What's that?" Juan asked.

"It's a pre-paid cell phone, so I don't have to come in here at this hour to talk to you."

"Cool!" said Juan as he grabbed the package and started opening it. He hesitated for a minute and he handed the package back to Collins. "I've been thinking. I don't know if I want to do this anymore. And I'm not sure I still want to be a cop."

Collins was surprised. "Kid, after what happened to your sister, you should be mad as hell and want to catch as many bad guys as you can."

"I am mad and I know it's going to take me a long time to get past this, but so what if we catch bad guys. The damage is already done. It won't undo any crime and it won't bring my sister back. All the victims still suffer. It doesn't change a thing."

"You're wrong, it changes a lot. Every criminal we put away stops five maybe ten crimes from happening. We're saving lots of people from ever becoming victims. We're doing a lot of good here, kid. You need to take some time and think about it. In the meantime, hold on to the phone and if you need to talk, call me."

"Okay. What's your number?"

"It's already programmed in. By the way, our friend the home invader tried to pull another job while we were watching him. He wasn't successful. Mr. Frizzano and his two partners are sitting comfortably in the lockup. Littlefield and I will be conducting interviews and organizing the facts of the case for the attorneys, and then we'll have to testify when the case comes up for trial. Other than that, the case is closed. So just take it easy and try to hold it together."

"I'll try."

Collins patted Juan on the shoulder and walked away.

Ken Morrison was at his desk on the other side of the squad room. He watched the exchange between Collins and Juan. Morrison thought it was odd that Collins was friendly with the help. Especially odd since the help wasn't a hot young female.

"Kind of a late night," Collins yelled to Morrison on his way out of the squad room.

"That's how it is when you have no life. By the way, good work on that Garret case. I wish I had your luck," Morrison yelled back.

"Thanks, but luck had nothing to do with it. Good night," said Collins and he left the room.

"Not luck, huh," mumbled Morrison under his breath. "I'll bet you had something working for ya."

CHAPTER TWENTY EIGHT

Sanders' day started off with a call from Detective John Smith of IA telling him that Joey Adams' car had been impounded and examined. There was blood found in the car along with Joey's and Eddie's prints. Since Eddie's prints were also found in the bloody stolen car, the blood samples from the two cars were compared and found to be the same type.

"Okay, we showed you ours and now you show us yours." Smith said. "What's all this have to do with Morrison?"

"It looks like Adams and Donovan stole a car and committed a liquor store heist. The crime was never reported. The next day, Morrison showed up at the store, stayed for about an hour and left with no purchase. He found and reviewed security camera footage of activity in front of the store. Next he showed up at Adams' aunt's house looking for him. A few days later, Adams and Donovan's bodies are found."

"What's your involvement?" asked Smith.

"We think Morrison is working for a heavy set gentleman who employed a person of interest. Both of whom have disappeared."

"That sounds real cloak and dagger. Do you have the name of this heavy gentleman?"

"Not yet, we're hoping the phone tap will provide the information we need. Has Morrison called anyone I would be interested in?" Sanders asked.

"Possibly, we picked up a call the other day that might be pertinent."

"Come on now, don't hold back. I just gave you a lead linking Morrison to two murders."

"Okay, Morrison put in a call to a guy named Omar, tipping him to the two bodies found in the park. He said that he'd follow the investigation and let Omar know what was happening."

"That's it! Did you get anything that would tell us who and where Omar is?"

"No, it was a call to a pre-paid phone. We could get you the number, but if you called it, that would tip them off."

"Right. I still don't have anything."

"What about that person of interest you mentioned?"

"All right, I'll tell you. His name is Azlan Yardim. He's here on an expired Visa and he's ex-military trained in Yemen. He was working in the liquor store the night of the robbery. Here's the deal. We are going to work together and play nice and you are going to get Morrison and I'm going to get Omar and Azlan. If you get Morrison and I don't get Omar and Azlan, I'm going to play my national security card. I will take Morrison from you and I'll give him a walk on the two murders and whatever else he's done if he can give me Omar. So help me get Omar or I'll see to it that you end up with nothing."

There was silence on the other end of the line for what seemed like five minutes.

"All right, we'll play nice." The call went on for another ten minutes. When everyone was finished speculating why the liquor store robbery had gone unreported, they agreed to a daily call to share information.

Omar arranged to meet with Anwar to check on his progress. The job that Anwar was setting up had the potential of adding hundreds of thousands to the group's war chest. Timing was important and so was the location. There were still too many unknowns.

"Have you identified the potential targets?" asked Omar.

"I have a number of targets, but unless I get more information, I can't say if they are good targets."

"What do you need?"

"I need to know my timetable, then I'll know if the bank is flush with cash or not."

"We have no control of the timetable. You've decided that it will be a bank?"

"Yes, Sterling Bank and Trust. They have six branches around the city, all with the exact same layout. We won't have to case the interiors of multiple sites. If the diversion is on the scale of 9/11, we won't have to worry about the police response time. We will be able to clean out the tellers' cages and force the manager to open the vault."

"That sounds good," said Omar.

"Everything still depends on the timetable. The more time we have to prepare, the better our chances for success."

"The only thing I can tell you about the timing is that our friends will enter the country tonight. Two will enter through Canada, the others through Mexico. They will be here by the end of the week to pick up the information, cash and equipment they need. The amount of cash I've been asked to provide them won't last too long, so I expect that they will complete their mission quickly."

"What about casualties in the bank? Should we try to limit casualties?"

"The people in the bank will dictate the casualty rate. If they cooperate, fine. If not, they'll be casualties. Don't hesitate to make an example of a few of them if necessary."

"I'm working with eight men as you directed. My plan only requires four."

"Continue working with all eight and consider the possibility of hitting two branches of the bank simultaneously. We'll talk again in a few days."

Anwar understood that the meeting had ended and he left the office.

CHAPTER TWENTY-NINE

Collins and Littlefield weren't called in to assist on the Wetlands Park double homicide; they were called to lead the investigation. They had impressed the right people with their recent successes. Their team included three investigators, a tech support guy and a behavioral psychologist who worked for the team part-time. They took over the conference room and the northeast corner of the squad room.

So far, they had identified the bodies as Edward Donovan and Joseph Adams. Both were small-time criminals with modest rap sheets. Each had spent time in the state penitentiary; Donovan had done a two-year stretch and Adams spent eighteen months there. Both were out on parole.

Each of the victims was shot twice in the back of the head execution style. Joseph Adams had also been shot in the kneecap. The slugs removed from the bodies were nine millimeter. Two different guns had been used. The assumption was that there were two shooters. There was facial bruising on both victims that appeared to have been done postmortem. Traces of saliva were also found on each body.

All the facts and photographs were carefully being laid out in the conference room. Team members had been dispatched to talk to the victims' parole officers and to talk to Estelle Adams. The parole officers were of no help. The victims had been checking in with their parole officers as required, but each lied about being employed. Ms. Estelle Adams, Joseph Adams' aunt, was helpful. She said that the victims had been reported as missing and the department had already sent people out to look for him. She said that they had impounded her nephew's car.

Littlefield pulled the missing persons reports for the two victims and handed a copy to Collins. "It looks like the department is stepping all over itself. Since when do you impound the car of a missing person?" asked Littlefield.

"Good question. Let's find out who authorized impounding the car."

Littlefield called the impound lot. After ten minutes on hold and a brief conversation with the lot supervisor, Littlefield found out that John Smith of Internal Affairs made the authorization request.

"What the hell does the rat squad have to do with this case?" Collins could see that this meant trouble for his investigation. "Anytime those assholes get involved, they get in the way and withhold evidence and generally screw things up."

"Those bastards won't tell us anything, but we have to ask them what they know."

Littlefield called John Smith and put him on speaker.

"This is Detective Smith."

"John, this is Littlefield and Collins from downstairs.

"Hey guys, what's up?"

"Hey John, we caught a double homicide case that happened up in Wetlands Park and it turns out that we have some overlap with a case you seem to be working on."

"Huh, what case is that?"

"Well, I don't know for sure, but one of our victims was Joey Adams. And it turns out that you had his car impounded the other day. Could you tell us what you're working on that concerns Adams?"

"Adams, yeah we're working on something that is unrelated to your homicide."

"How do you know it's unrelated? Tell us what you got and we'll decide if it's unrelated."

"You guys know the sensitive nature of our cases. We can't risk compromising our investigation. But we'll share everything we got from the car."

"Why were you looking at Adams and his car in the first place?"

"Can't tell you that, but I'm sending you the forensic report we got."

"Damn-it, Smith. You better not obstruct our investigation!"

"I wouldn't think of it."

"If you're not going to help, you better stay the hell out of the way." Collins pressed the speaker button harder than he needed to and the call ended. "That piece of shit; we'd better tell the brass about this little complication."

"They won't do anything; they don't have any control over IA."

"I know, but they need to be told, and we need to cover our asses in case IA screws up our case."

CHAPTER THIRTY

Omar carefully placed the envelope and the cash in his briefcase. They wanted the envelope, and he was going to make sure that they got it. He was a valued member of the group, but not valuable enough to get away with making mistakes. He left word that he would be gone for the rest of the day and walked out.

It was a nice day for this time of the year in southern Florida. Anything below 90 degrees in July is considered nice. Omar got in his car and headed for the highway. The interstate was crowded as usual, but traffic was flowing. He reached his exit in 35 minutes and followed the signs pointing downtown. He passed through the center of the city and went to the warehouse district.

He found the address he was looking for. It was a large warehouse complex of at least ten buildings. He entered the proper code on the keypad at the gate and it slowly opened. He drove to building seven and parked. He used the key he had been sent to open the door and he walked in, unarmed. Omar had done this before; in the past, he just left the cash or papers in a desk drawer and went home.

This time, he expected to meet the people he was dealing with. He was right. Four men were on the warehouse floor and they ushered him into the office. "Welcome, Brother," one of the men said smiling. "I am Turhan."

Omar had decided not to look like a vulnerable deliveryman, but to take control. He wanted to give the impression of being part of the operation, not a potential loose end. "I brought what was asked for." He opened his case and handed Turhan a sealed envelope with the sheet of codes. "There's no need for further introductions. It is best that we know as little as possible about each other."

"What about weapons?" one of the men asked.

"The weapons will be delivered before they are needed. If there is a need, I can supply them with four hours' notice. My people and I will do whatever is necessary to support you and ensure your success."

"We were told that you could be trusted, so I will tell you. Against my wishes, we were told to use multiple support groups in case one is discovered or unable to obtain what we need. The other group is behind schedule. We will wait another day for them to show up. If they don't, you will also need to provide vehicles for us."

"That is not a problem. I can provide everything."

"You don't need to provide anything else. The Russians have provided the device."

"Turhan, shut up," one of the others said. "You always talk too much. The weapons and the vehicles will be all we need from you, Brother Omar."

"Just tell me when and where you want them delivered." Omar said.

One of the other men produced a list of weapons and handed it to Omar. "We will let you know when we need delivery."

Omar said his goodbyes. He held his breath as he walked out of the warehouse. In these dealings, he was never sure that he was going to be able to walk away safely. After he made it back to his car, Omar started to process the information he was given:

The Russians have provided the 'device'; all they needed now was weapons and vehicles; and The Envelope was crucial to the operation.

Omar had more information than he wanted. Now, he had to develop new plans.

As he drove back to the office he called Anwar from his cell phone and told him that they needed to meet. Anwar was waiting outside the auto body shop when Omar pulled up. "Our timetable just got changed."

"Do you know when it will happen?"

Omar walked Anwar to the office, entered and closed the door. "I know everything. Now we need to make sure it doesn't happen."

"What do you mean?" asked Anwar.

"We're being set up.

"Set up? What do you mean?"

"I'll explain. The organization planned an operation that had four people smuggled into the country to set off explosives and four suicide bombs in and around a facility that I assume is Hutchinson Island Nuclear Power Plant."

"So what's the problem?"

"They are not suicide bombers, it's a suicide mission. Something about the mission bothered me. I couldn't put my finger on it until now. They aren't planning another 9/11, they're planning to trigger another Chernobyl. They slipped up and told me that the Russians are providing the device, not explosives. The codes in the letter I delivered are access codes to the device. They are going to use a nuclear bomb. And we here in Port St. Lucie are in the kill zone."

"That can't be."

"They are using a nuclear device to blow up a nuclear facility. If we are not killed by the blast, the radiation will surely kill us; it might take us years to die. Any way you look at it, we are being sacrificed."

"How can they do that? Why wouldn't they warn us to leave the area?"

"It might raise suspicion. I don't know. Maybe they don't think we are that valuable. The mission is an important one. If it is successful, it might help us win the war at home and demoralize the country here. One thing is certain. We can stop planning our bank robberies; nobody's going to be left to count the money."

"Why would they betray us? We've always been loyal, we've always supported them."

"We support them, but we're not one of them; that makes us expendable."

"No, that makes them expendable."

"Easy, Anwar, we're still on the same side. We can't challenge them directly."

"Are we going to sit back and do nothing?"

"No, we have to foil their operation without being involved. We have to have a third party deliver the weapons and cars while we tip the feds to the whereabouts of our four friends."

"One of the east coast gangs could make the delivery, but they would balk if they suspected they were dealing with terrorists. The fools get continually screwed by this country, yet they still remain patriots. Our mid-west militia gun customer would be a better choice. The moment the feds showed themselves, those crazy idiots would open fire. If we're lucky, no one would come out alive." Anwar grinned as he talked.

"That could work. We'll offer our militia friends a discount on their next gun shipment if they handle the delivery for us," said Omar.

"How do we provide information to the Feds?"

"Simple, have our men use throw away cell phones and make the call near a Mosque south of the city. The cell towers near any sizable Mosque are monitored. Tell them to speak Farsi and to say: 'The attack is imminent and the details will be provided'. The call will alert the Feds and they'll be ready when our second call gives them the time and location of the delivery."

CHAPTER THIRTY-ONE

Sanders' call with Internal Affairs was short. IA's tail on Morrison was not producing anything and there had been no more calls to Omar. "Morrison is not going to call Omar until he has something to tell him. How's the murder investigation proceeding?" asked Sanders.

"We're not directly involved," said Smith.

"You need to get involved! You need to help the investigation along. If there's progress, Morrison will make contact with Omar."

"What can we do?"

"You can squeeze Morrison. Tell the cops that you showed old lady Adams a picture of Morrison and she identified him as the guy who was looking for Donovan and Adams before they were found murdered. When Morrison finds out that he's part of the investigation, he'll panic and run to Omar."

"Did she actually identify him?"

"Yes she did. Don't worry; I'm not trying to set him up. He fingered those punks for Omar and he got them killed."

"Okay, I'll help the detectives tie Morrison to their investigation; but they won't take it well. They'll accuse IA of holding out on them. It won't help our already strained relationship."

"Since when has IA worried about their relationship with the rank and file?"

"It may not look like it, but we do try to work with those guys."

"You work with them to try and nail their brethren. You know that you're never going to get any big wet kisses from those guys. Be satisfied with getting rid of the scum when you can."

"All right, all right, I'll tell them what they need to know."

The conference room was covered with crime scene photographs and post-it notes, time line charts, maps, forensic reports, everything that had to do with the double homicide in Wetlands Park. Juan was in the room trying to take it all in when Collins and Littlefield came in. "How are you doing?" Collins couldn't think of anything better to say.

"I'm very sorry for your loss." Littlefield added.

"Thank you. I've decided that my dad was right, it's better to keep busy than to sit and think about my personal problems. I've been looking at all the evidence that's been gathered. It's a lot to digest. There's obviously a personal element," said Juan, using a phrase from one of his textbooks. "The way they abused the victims by kicking and spitting on them, that's personal."

"Murderers generally don't like their victims." Littlefield couldn't resist mocking the kid.

Juan went on, ignoring him, "One of the victims was tortured, suggesting that he knew something the killers wanted to know, or he was being punished for something he did, or both. I assume you're trying to get a DNA sample from the saliva on the victims."

"Yeah, they're testing the spit as we speak."

"The forensic report on the car says that the blood found didn't belong to either of the victims. Maybe the victims hurt someone and they retaliated. If the lab can tell how old the blood is, then the hospitals could be checked to see if anyone was admitted around that time with severe blood loss."

"That's paper thin, but it's something," said Littlefield, not impressed with Juan's efforts. "Keep working on it, kid. Something will pop out of that big brain of yours. We'll be checking in with you."

With that, Collins and Littlefield headed for the elevator. They made it down to the lobby when Collins' cell phone started ringing. He flipped it open. "This is Detective Collins."

"Collins, John Smith here. Sorry about the late call, but I have something you should know."

"No problem. What have you got?" Collins pressed the speakerphone button on his cell.

"One of my guys interviewed your victim's aunt a week or so ago and he showed her a picture of Detective Ken Morrison. She identified Morrison as a man who had come to her house looking for Donovan and Adams. I know you probably interviewed her already, but it occurred to me that if you didn't show her the picture, she probably didn't tell you about Morrison."

"It just occurred to you that this might be important?"

"Well we were looking at things from a different perspective. We're following a bad cop and you're looking for a murderer."

"You son of a bitch, why..."

"Easy, easy, we didn't think it was that important because we verified that Morrison had an alibi for the time of the murders."

"You still should have told us. Is there anything else you're holding back?"

"No, that's all we have. Be a pal and don't let Morrison know that we're watching him."

"Yeah right, you can count on me." Collins hung up. He and Littlefield began to speculate about Morrison's involvement.

"We've got to get Morrison in the interrogation room and find out everything he knows."

"Is it better to go at Morrison head on, or to quietly investigate him?"

"IA has been investigating him quietly. If those bastards haven't found out enough to charge him with something, quiet is not the way to go." Collins did have an idea. "Just to be safe, let's get a picture of Morrison and visit the aunt before we talk to him."

A few hours later, Collins and Littlefield knocked on Ms. Adams' front door. It was much too early for Ms. Adams to be in a cheery mood. "What the hell do you want?" she shouted.

"Ma'am, we're from the police department and we need to ask you a few questions."

"More questions, I got a question for you. Did you find out who killed my nephew?"

"We're trying…"

"You're trying my patience. What do you want to know now?"

"Have you ever seen this man?" Collins handed her the photograph of Morrison.

"Him again, don't you guys talk to each other? Yeah I saw him. He came here looking for Joey and Eddie. He said it had something to do with insurance. What else do you want to know?"

"That's all. Thank you."

"Go do your job and leave me alone." She slammed the door shut.

Littlefield looked at Collins, "I guess that gets rid of any doubts I might have had about Morrison's involvement, if I had any."

CHAPTER THIRTY-TWO

Back in the office, Morrison and his partner, Ann Howard, were lamenting their unsolved burglary case. "We're nowhere on this thing. We haven't even got a suspect." Morrison was flipping through the case file. "We've looked as hard as you can at the victims. They weren't in on it."

"It looks like this one is going to be filed away as unsolved." Ann slumped down in her chair.

"We're going to have to close a case soon. I've heard a rumor that the brass is considering busting some detectives back to patrol. I look like shit in a uniform."

"The atmosphere is really tense around here since the superstars started closing cases left and right. Those guys and their new CI have really screwed things up for the rest of us."

"CI my ass." Morrison scowled, "They've got a secret weapon, but it's not a CI."

"What makes you say that?"

"The cases they closed were nothing alike. A CI has a specialty. Either they know about drug deals or jewelry heists or maybe they have some information about a specific crime if someone's on the street shooting his mouth off. But no CI knows about different types of crimes occurring in different parts of the city. They don't have a CI, they have a psychic."

"Well if that's what they got, we need one too."

Morrison thought back and remembered the late night encounter between Collins and the janitor's kid. He thought it was funny at the time. *'No, that's ridiculous, how could a kid know anything?'* Morrison turned his attention back to the open file on his desk and Howard wandered off toward the common coffee pot.

Collins and Littlefield entered the squad room. Everyone saw them come in and watched as they walked to their desks. It seemed to Morrison that they were looking at him. They weren't staring, but Morrison was sure that they were focused on him. Collins sat down at his desk and said, "How do you want to do this? Should we tell him to call his union rep to come and sit in on the interview or should we have an informal chat."

"I'm thinking that we start out chatting. There's always time for formalities later on. We just have a couple of questions. If we get the wrong answers, then he can lawyer up."

"That's the way I want to play it too. I'll see if there's a free interrogation room, you invite him to join us."

Littlefield poured himself a cup of coffee and walked over to Morrison's desk. "Morning, Ken. How's it going?"

"A visit from one of the men of the hour. To what do I owe this honor?"

"You know we caught the double homicide in the park. Collins and I want to run a few things by you to sort of pick your brain. Have you got a minute?"

"Yeah sure, I'm real curious about that case. Two small time guys executed and dumped in the park like that. Sure, I got time."

Collins was waiting in interrogation room two. "Morning, Ken. How ya doing?"

"Fine. Why don't we talk in the conference room?"

said Morrison.

"There are too many distractions in there. We only have a couple of specific questions."

"Fire away." Morrison seemed calm, but he was beginning to get a little apprehensive.

Collins started talking. "When we were interviewing people who knew the victims, we came across something odd. A family member of one of the victims said that you were looking for Adams and Donovan about a week before the murders. Can you tell us what that's all about?"

Morrison felt as though he'd been kicked in the gut, but he quickly composed himself. "I was looking at those guys in connection with a burglary that I'm working."

"What pointed you to those guys?" Littlefield was taking in every eye movement and twitch that Morrison made.

"They were small time thieves recently out of the joint. I was just touching all the bases."

"Did you know that they had never been charged with a burglary?"

"The fact that they'd never been charged with one doesn't mean that they never committed one. Hey, are you guys accusing me of something?"

"Of course not. We just find it a little odd that out of the blue, another detective pops up in the middle of our investigation. You could have told us about your connection when we caught the case and the bodies were identified."

"There was no connection, I never found them."

"Do you still think they were involved in your burglary case?"

"No, it was just a hunch that didn't pan out. You got any more questions?" Morrison was clearly agitated.

"No, that's it Ken. Thanks for your time." Collins opened the interrogation room door and Morrison quickly left.

Collins looked at Littlefield, "It looks like there's a lot he's not telling us."

Back at his desk, Morrison was about to explode. His heart was pounding and his blood pressure was off the scale. He couldn't wait to call Omar. But he had to wait. He decided to call at 10:00 am. At 10:00 am every morning, everyone working on the double homicide met in the conference room to go over their status. No one would notice him making his call. For forty-five minutes he tried to appear interested in his burglary file. When the crowd started working their way into the conference room, he headed out to the parking lot to make the call from his car.

It was warm outside. *"It's ten o'clock in the morning and it's already eighty-five degrees."* Morrison was irritated and everything was pissing him off. He decided to stand outside the car to make the call.

"This is Omar."

"Omar, we've got a problem."

"It seems like I've heard this before. What's the problem now?"

"They're on to me. They found out I talked to the old lady, Joey's aunt."

"How did they do that? Did you leave a card with the old lady?"

"No, I wouldn't do anything that stupid. I don't know

how they did it."

"All you have to do is keep your mouth shut. So what if you talked to the old lady? There's no crime in that."

"Yeah, I know. I told them I talked to her in connection with another case I'm working on. But they never should have been able to find me. I never gave her my real name. They must have shown her a picture of me."

"How would they know to do that?" Omar was beginning to think that Morrison had lost it.

"I've got an idea, but you'll think it's crazy."

"What is it?"

"I think they're using a psychic."

"A psychic?"

"Hear me out. The detectives on this case are second rate. They've been doing average work for years. Suddenly, they started clearing all the cases that are thrown at them. They are handed this case, a double homicide and somehow they found out about me. The other night, I saw one of them talking to a kid who does janitorial work at the station. They were real buddy buddy. I think the kid is giving them tips, pointing them in the right direction. I can't prove it yet, but I think the kid is the key to their success."

"You're right; I do think you're crazy. A psychic, that's nonsense. Just stay calm and watch them. The case will hit a dead end soon and that will be the end of it."

"Okay, I'll continue to keep an eye on things. By the way, I think it's time I got paid again. Where are you now? Why don't I drop by your place later today?"

"Not a good idea if you think they're on to you. I'll put something in the mail for you. Call me if you have anything worthwhile to report." Omar hung up. He rocked his desk chair back and forth.

"Do we have a problem?" Hassan was sitting in a guest chair and had listened to one side of the phone conversation.

"I have to keep reminding myself that Morrison is a trained detective and that his information is valuable. Now he thinks the cops are using a janitor psychic to help solve their cases. If he doesn't settle down, he could have an accident, a bad one."

Morrison put his phone in his pocket and went back in the building. On his way in, he passed by the receptionist's desk. Linda was thirty-one, pleasant looking with a nice personality. Her only goal was to find a non-policeman husband. "Hey Linda, do you know the janitor, George?"

"Yes, I've met him. Nice man."

"His kid works here with him. Do you know his name?"

"It's Juan, Juan Santos, a good kid, very polite. He just graduated from high school."

"Juan, I'll remember that. Thanks. Have a good day."

Morrison still had no idea he was being followed by IA, but after the questioning by Collins and Littlefield, his antennae were up. He looked up the address of George Santos. His plan was to track Juan Santos' movements and to learn his schedule. If it became necessary, he'd be ready to dispose of the superstars' secret weapon before Juan Santos became more of a problem.

CHAPTER THIRTY-THREE

The meeting in the conference room turned out to be a re-hash of the facts that everyone already knew. The bullets dug out of the victims were in good enough shape to be matched to a gun if one was ever found. The DNA from the spit was not on file, but it was ready to be matched to a suspect if one was ever found. There was no mention of Morrison or the conversations with Internal Affairs.

Collins and Littlefield had assigned people to profile the victims. The profiles were shared at the meeting and they turned out to be a sad tale of two underachievers who drank, did drugs and stole whatever they could. The victims had no friends and no current girlfriends. And most of their known associates were in the joint.

The detectives also had people canvas the area hospitals looking for anyone who was admitted with severe blood loss around the time that the murders occurred. The canvassers reported that there were three incidents in which the patient had substantial blood loss, two stabbings and one shooting that led nowhere.

An orderly did tell a canvasser that a nurse found her car with blood on the seats. The nurse was interviewed and told the canvasser that the police were called and the car was impounded. The canvassers looked up the incident report on the nurse's stolen car and found the fingerprint connection to Edward Donovan.

"Great work!" said Collins. "They stole a car before they were murdered. They also returned the car to the same location."

Someone in the back of the room said, "I'll bet they stole the car to commit a robbery and returned back to pick up their own car."

"We need to find out what robberies were reported on the night the car was stolen." Littlefield sat down at the table and opened his PC. He pounded on a few keys, moved his fingers over the touchpad and sighed, "No robberies reported."

"Crap." Collins couldn't hold back his frustration. "I was sure we were on the right track."

The meeting went on for another hour with no progress. The conference room whiteboard was updated with the new information and the meeting was adjourned.

It was Sanders' turn to call Internal Affairs. He hoped there would be some results from the tail on Morrison, but he wasn't going to hold his breath. "Good morning, John. Anything happening?"

"We just intercepted a call to Omar. We'll have a transcript sent to you in a few minutes."

"Was anything important said?"

"The lead detectives told Morrison that they found out that he had talked to the old lady. He tried to put them off with a lie about working on another case. He somehow got the idea that the detectives have a psychic working for them. He also thinks that the psychic is the night shift janitor."

"What did Omar say?"

"He said that he thought Morrison was crazy. He told Morrison to keep his mouth shut and that there would be something in the mail for him."

"Do you plan to intercept that mailing?"

"Absolutely. We'll go over it with a fine-tooth comb and send it on to Morrison. I don't expect Omar to put a return address on it, but some DNA would be nice."

"Anything else?" asked Sanders.

"Morrison asked Omar for his location and offered to drop by to pick up his money. So we know that Morrison doesn't know Omar's address. One more thing, I've only heard Omar's voice twice, but there was something in the way he spoke that suggested that Morrison had better watch his step. If Morrison's smart, he picked it up too."

"It sounds like you need to watch Morrison closely. You can't prosecute a dead cop."

"We'll watch him all right; this psychic talk is not good. If he thinks the janitor is fingering him, he might try to hurt the guy."

"I guess stranger things have happened. I'll talk to you tomorrow."

CHAPTER THIRTY-FOUR

Omar waited patiently for the call that would set the delivery time for the terrorists' equipment. Anwar had arranged for the third party to be ready to deliver the guns and vehicles to the warehouse. The third party was six members of the Wilaree Militia who were enticed to participate with the promise of discounts on future arms shipments. Anwar also had one of his men watching the warehouse and another man ready to tip off the Feds.

Omar's plan for dealing with the terrorists had been examined from every angle. The ATF would be alerted to the arms deal. None of Omar's men would be directly involved; and none of the survivors, if any, would know any details about Omar's cell. The only casualty was Omar's plan to use the terrorist act as a diversion to commit one or two profitable robberies.

"It would have been beautiful. We could have walked away with hundreds of thousands and it would have been days before they would have bothered to start looking for us."

"Yes, it is a shame. It was a good plan." Anwar was happy that the robbery would not take place. He never thought of himself as a common thief.

The phone rang. Omar answered it, mumbled a few confirming words and hung up. "It's set for ten o'clock tomorrow morning."

Anwar called his man and told him to go to the Mosque and make the call that would tip the Feds to the time and place of the delivery.

Omar put his hand on Anwar's arm. "Tell the delivery guys to be careful. Tell them that there shouldn't be any problems since this is only a delivery and no money is changing hands. But be sure to tell them that no one is to be trusted."

"I'll tell them what they need to know," said Anwar, as he walked out. When he got to his car, he pulled out his cell phone and called his man watching the warehouse. "Shayan, what is going on at the warehouse?"

"There's been no movement."

"The delivery is set for 10 am Monday morning. Get there at nine. Find a good location where you can't be spotted and set up. Make sure that the four traitors in the warehouse don't survive. You can take out the deliverymen if you have time, but avoid hitting the cops."

"It will be done." Shayan signed off.

Juan suffered through the worst Fourth of July weekend in his life. Rose's funeral was held on the fourth. George and Marie thought about moving the date of the ceremony, but they decided that Saturday was the right day. They wanted the people whose lives she touched to always remember her. Holding the funeral on the fourth was one way to do it. Juan knew that this holiday would become a day of mourning every year for the rest of his life. He couldn't stand to see his mother cry, and she cried all weekend.

He spent as much time as he could by himself. He was in too much pain to be a comfort to anyone else. He was filled with rage and hatred for the criminal who was responsible for the loss of his sister, a sister that he ignored and avoided whenever he could, a sister that he loved with all his heart. He focused on his anger and it helped with the pain. He considered going to Fort Lauderdale and offering to help with the hijacking case. But he knew that was ridiculous; they'd laugh him out of the police station. And Collins and Littlefield wouldn't back him up. He felt helpless, and he was.

Juan thought about Collins' words. He knew it was just a pep talk to try and boost his spirits, but it was true. *"Every criminal taken off the streets reduces the number of future victims."*

He had to admit that he never cared about victims before. His desire to become a policeman was all about outsmarting the criminals. It was all just a game. Now that he had become a victim, it was no longer a game.

The weekend seemed like it lasted forever, but it was finally over. Juan was looking forward to getting back to the job he hated. George and Juan rode to work in silence. They hadn't had much to say to each other since Rose died. Juan thought his father was disappointed in him for not being more of a comfort to his mother and little sister. And he was looking for any excuse he could find to be mad at his father. He thought about the years he still was going to have to help the family pay for a wedding and now a funeral.

Juan turned and looked at his father and his anger subsided. Sitting behind the steering wheel, George looked smaller. He looked tired and his shoulders were stooped. He realized that he had no right to direct his anger toward his father. George had suffered enough. As they left the car and entered the building, Juan put his arm on George's shoulder and said, "Have a good day, Dad."

"You too, Son." George walked away looking a bit less like an old man.

Juan did his grunt work quickly and an hour and forty-five minutes later, he was looking over the updated whiteboard in the conference room. He paid special attention to the note that said that Donovan and Adams stole a car before they were killed and the theory was that they stole it to commit a crime. That fit with Juan's idea that Adams was tortured in order to get some information or items that the killer wanted. Based on their records, Donovan and Adams stole money or jewelry; and Juan suspected that this time they stole from the wrong people.

Juan was anxious to try out his new phone. He hit speed dial #1.

"This is Don Collins."

"Detective Collins, this is Juan Santos.'

"I know, Juan. I have caller ID. Do you have something for me?"

"I'm not sure. I just want to run a few things by you."

"Shoot."

"First of all, is what you've got in the conference room all the information you have?"

"Yeah that's it, but the case is still developing."

"Okay, it seems like there are pieces missing."

"I'm sure there are. Like who killed the guys, why were they killed, etc?"

"That's not what I mean. I'll explain in a minute. What I've got is a theory that the victims stole a car to commit a robbery and they were successful. But they made the mistake of stealing from the wrong people. Whatever they stole was important enough that the robbery victim had to get it back. Also, whatever was stolen couldn't be reported to the police. So the robbery victims found Donovan and Adams on their own, tortured them until they returned the stolen items and killed them."

"That sounds plausible."

"Yeah, except for one thing. How could the robbery victim find the robbers without using the police? Who has the resources to find people like that? Unless Donovan and Adams left their IDs at the crime scene, I don't know how they could have been found."

"Neither do I," said Collins. "That little exception sort of destroys your theory, doesn't it?"

"No, it just hurts it a little. There's one more thing. The murder victims left blood in the stolen car that wasn't theirs. I think that they hurt someone bad when they committed the robbery. Since the check of the hospitals for a severe bleeding victim didn't pan out, maybe they killed someone when they committed the robbery. And maybe part of the reason for their murders was payback."

"A lot of maybes."

"If I could just figure out how Donovan and Adams were found by the killers."

"Keep at it, kid. I'll talk to you later." Collins hung up chuckling to himself. He got some perverse pleasure from jerking Juan around. He had to remember to tell Littlefield how he held back the Morrison information from Juan. Nobody wanted to let the kid get a swelled head. Best to keep him humble as long as they could.

Collins knew that the kid had done it again. Morrison must have fingered Donovan and Adams for the mysterious robbery victim. The next step would be to put a tail on Morrison and to tap his phones, but Collins knew that he didn't have enough evidence to get a court order for a tap. He knew IA was watching Morrison. Knowing IA, they probably already had a tap on him.

The phone call with Collins left Juan a little uneasy. He was sure his theories had merit. He went about his work too distracted to notice Morrison staring into the conference room through the glass door. The door opened and Morrison stepped in. Juan looked up. "Hi."

"Hi kid, I'm Detective Morrison. Juan is it?"

"Yes, sir."

"You probably already know, but I wanted to tell you to be careful in here. The stuff on the boards is for an on-going investigation and it shouldn't be disturbed."

"Yes, sir, I know. I'm always very careful when I work in here."

"Be sure that you are. You could find yourself in a lot of trouble if you meddle where you don't belong. Do you understand what I'm telling you?"

"Yes, I won't disturb anything."

"Good, I'm glad we understand each other. Hey, you look kind of familiar. My name is Morrison. Have you heard of me?"

"No, I don't think so."

"Have you ever been in trouble with the law?"

"No, sir, no way."

"Good, keep your nose clean. I'll be keeping an eye on you."

"Good night, sir."

Morrison left feeling a little better. The kid wasn't all-seeing and all-knowing. The kid didn't react at all when he told him who he was. Either the kid was a great actor or he had never heard the name Morrison before. He decided to back off and watch things from a distance and continue to track the kid's movements. He walked out of the building into the warm, humid, night air. His glasses fogged up and he stopped to wipe them with his handkerchief. In the parking lot, he got the feeling that he wasn't alone. He glanced around the lot, but he didn't see anyone. Morrison checked his watch. It was almost 1:00 AM. There was still time for a drink or two at his neighborhood bar before turning in.

CHAPTER THIRTY-FIVE

Years of military training taught Shayan to be on time for all operations. He showed up before nine and settled himself in the position he had selected the night before. He was on a neighboring office building five hundred yards from the warehouse. From his vantage point, he could see everything surrounding the warehouse.

At nine thirty, four black vans pulled up and parked on a side street three blocks from the warehouse. Several men in combat gear with sniper rifles stepped out and ran to nearby buildings. Moments later they appeared on the roofs approximately two hundred yards from the warehouse. Everyone was in Shayan's field of fire and his Parker-Hale M85 had never failed him before.

The delivery vehicles arrived on time and pulled up to the front gate. The gate slowly opened and the vehicles, two vans and a sedan, drove to the warehouse. The warehouse door opened and the vans drove inside. The law enforcement vehicles started moving down the side street toward the lot entrance. The black vans reached the front gate and rammed it. The vans raced to the warehouse door and took up positions on either side of the entrance.

Shayan could see the law enforcement officers cover the sedan in front of the warehouse, pointing heavy weapons at the windows. A minute later, they pulled two deliverymen out. "So much for the fierce, cop hating militia men," Shayan muttered to himself.

After the two deliverymen were secured, law

enforcement spread out and took positions covering the warehouse windows and exits. Shayan was too far away to hear anything, but he was sure that the usual surrender or else negotiations were taking place. Everyone held his position for what seemed like a long time. Shayan could barely make out the letters on the back of the sniper nearest him. There were three letters, not FBI; it was ATF.

Shayan was not impressed with the ATF so far. He thought it was stupid for them to let the weapons get into the warehouse. Now the ATF had all the bad guys together in the warehouse with more firepower than they had before.

Shayan heard the sound of muffled gunfire. The ATF gunmen ducked and or flinched, but Shayan didn't see any muzzle flashes. The gunfire was coming from inside the warehouse. The ATF fired gas canisters through the warehouse windows and positioned themselves to breach the warehouse. The warehouse door opened and men began to rush out.

From his position, Shayan wasn't able to tell if the men coming out were the terrorists or the militia. He waited until six of them cleared the door and opened fire. He had a bolt-action sniper rifle and he was only able to shoot three before the ATF snipers located his position and began to return fire.

Shayan had no choice but to turn his weapon on the ATF snipers. They were below him and the sun was at his back. They didn't have a chance. Remembering his instructions, Shayan shot them both in the chest. If they followed protocol and wore vests, they would be taken out of commission, but not seriously hurt.

Shayan turned his attention back to the front of the warehouse. The ATF had forced all the warehouse combatants to the ground and were covering them with their weapons. He counted seven men on the ground four spread eagle and three sprawled. Shayan fired four more times and began to dismantle his weapon. The ATF agents on the ground finally realized that the sniper wasn't theirs and they scattered for cover. Shayan exited the building, got in his car and followed his planned route out of the area. He couldn't be sure the four terrorists were dead, but he had done all he could.

Collins delayed his morning staff meeting until the afternoon in order to pass on Juan's theory to Littlefield. "Everything seems to fit. Morrison is working for the killers."

"If he didn't have an alibi for the time of the murders, I would have thought he did it."

"Too bad we can't charge him for it and sweat him until he gives up his employer."

"We've got a great theory; we just can't prove any of it."

"You know, Juan said something to me last night. He didn't know that I was holding out on him, but he did know something was missing. He asked me if all the evidence was here. That was a good question. IA has been giving us bits of information. I wonder if they're holding out on us. Let's ask them." Collins dialed the number.

"Internal Affairs, John Smith."

"Smith, this is Collins."

"Good morning, Don. How's it going?"

"Let's cut the small talk. I think we've almost caught

up with you guys. Our homicide victims committed a robbery, but they robbed the wrong people. Morrison was called in to find the robbers. He found them and they were killed. Now tell us what other information you have."

"That's it. You know everything we know."

"I doubt it. What aren't you telling us?"

"Trust me. We're not holding out on you. That's all we got."

"I know you've been tailing Morrison and you have probably been tapping his phones. Either you tell me everything or we'll sit Morrison down and tell him about your tail and tap. We'll also tell the brass that you're guilty of obstruction. I think they'll listen. I'm pretty sure a double homicide trumps a dirty cop investigation."

"Okay, okay, relax. We don't have that much more than you. We believe that your murder victims held up a liquor store on the east side of town. We can't prove anything, it was never reported. Since the murders, Morrison has been calling someone called Omar, informing him about the progress on the case."

"Who is this Omar? What's his address?"

"We don't know anything about Omar. It looks like he ordered the murders after he got his property back."

"What pointed you to Morrison in the first place?"

"There was a security video taken across the street from the liquor store. Morrison was on it, showing up the next day, spending time in the store and not buying anything."

"What else do you know?"

"That's it, except that Omar's not happy with Morrison. On the last call, Morrison told Omar that you guys had a psychic working for you."

"Bullshit."

"No shit. He said the janitor's kid was a psychic and he's been helping you solve cases. He told Omar that if the kid was taken care of, all their problems would go away."

"What did Omar say?"

"He told Morrison that he was crazy and to lay low and keep his mouth shut. That's all we got."

"All right, we'll keep your tail and tap to ourselves. Don't hold out on us anymore." Collins hung up and turned to Littlefield. "We've got to keep our own eye on Morrison."

"And no more keeping Juan in the dark about Morrison." Littlefield didn't say anything, but he liked Juan. If he got hurt as a result of his working on cases, there would be severe consequences for anyone who hurt him. "I think I should have a word with Morrison."

"What about?"

"I won't blow IA's tail or tap. I think we need to put pressure on him. If he gets agitated enough, he'll call Omar. If we can get Omar to make a move on Morrison, we might be able to pick Omar up. At the very least, we'll get Morrison to turn on him."

"That's a good idea. Let him know that we can't come after him officially yet, but you've got a hunch he's dirty and you're going to prove it."

Shayan didn't like to use his cell phone while he was driving, but called Anwar from the car. "It went down."

"Did you get all four?"

"I can't be absolutely sure. I got seven. The delivery people may have handled one or two of the original four."

"I don't understand, but I can wait until you get here." Anwar signed off. He didn't want the details of the shooting discussed over a cell phone. He was confident that he had made the right decision to use Shayan without discussing it with Omar. Omar could have said no and that would have been a mistake. Anwar turned on the local news channel and waited for Shayan.

Twenty minutes later, Shayan showed up at Anwar's place, a two-bedroom apartment. The place was clean and sparsely furnished. There were no pictures of family or friends and no mementos that Shayan could see. It looked like a place that could be abandoned in a minute, leaving no trace of the owner behind. Anwar let him in and led him into the living room. "What happened?"

"Those ATF idiots let the delivery take place in the warehouse, then surrounded it. I couldn't see what was going on. ATF closed in and started negotiating and I heard gunfire coming from inside the warehouse. ATF used teargas and men came out of the warehouse. As they came out, I opened fire. I put down the seven who came out."

"Did you kill any cops?"

"No, but I had to shoot the snipers in their vests. They may have a few broken ribs but that's all."

"We should be all right. None of them knew the details of Omar's cell. The four only knew Omar's name and how to contact him. All we can do now is to see what the reporters have to say."

CHAPTER THIRTY-SIX

John Smith initiated the call to Agent Sanders. "We've got no news for you, Sanders. No new calls to Omar."

"That's just as well; we've just been put on alert. ATF tried to take down an arms sale between a terror cell and some militia group. The operation was a bust and eight bad guys got killed. The ATF are a bunch of morons."

"Okay, if you're busy, we won't keep you. Just to let you know, we did have to come clean with the homicide detectives. We confirmed our tap and our search for Omar. We knew that we had to tell them everything eventually."

"Did you tell them about the FBI's interest?"

"No, you and the bureau were not part of the discussion."

"Good," said Sanders. "Call you tomorrow." He turned his attention to his computer screen and the reports that were coming in about the ATF bust.

Littlefield tried to script his upcoming conversation with Morrison. He and Collins had put Morrison on guard with their interview, so subtlety was not going to be the proper approach. Littlefield was also royally pissed to think that Morrison might try to hurt Juan. The more he thought about it, the more pissed he got. He walked over to Morrison's desk. He put his palms on the desk and leaned in and quietly said, "Collins thinks you're dirty. I think you're dirty. And if anything happens to Juan Santos, I'll put two in the back of your head." Littlefield's smile had nothing to do with humor. He pushed off Morrison's desk and walked back to the conference room.

Collins was sitting at the conference table going over his notes when Littlefield walked in. "I'm pretty sure that I got the message across to Morrison. He'll be making that call to Omar soon."

"Good, the sooner we get that bum in cuffs the better."

"I think we'd better make a call too." He hit the speakerphone and dialed the number.

"Hello."

"Good morning, Juan, I hope we didn't wake you. This is Littlefield and Collins."

"Good morning, did something happen?"

"No, not yet. We just wanted to fill you in on the case. We have an update for you. It seems that the people who were robbed by Donovan and Adams contacted a police detective to help them search for the robbers."

"A detective? Who was it?"

"His name is Detective Ken Morrison. It looks like he was working for the people who tortured and killed Donovan and Adams."

There was silence on the line. "Juan, did you hear me?"

"Yes. Detective Morrison was with me last night in the conference room."

Collins and Littlefield stared at each other. "What did he do? What did he say?"

"He told me to be careful and not disturb any of the evidence. I told him that I knew to be careful. He told me I could get into trouble if I meddled where I don't belong. Then he told me his name and he asked me if I knew him or heard his name before. I said 'no'. Then he told me to keep my nose clean and that he was keeping an eye on me. That was it; then he said 'goodnight'. He was kind of scary and weird. What does my nose have to do with anything?"

"Don't worry about it; it's just an old expression." If Morrison ever comes near you again, let us know right away. He's a bad guy fishing for information."

"Okay, I'll be sure to let you know."

"Yeah, go back to sleep. We'll be talking to you." Littlefield turned off the speakerphone. He was red with rage. "I'm going to kill that son of a bitch."

"Calm down. Now that he knows we're on to him, he wouldn't dare go after Juan."

"I don't care if IA already has a tail on him; I'm going to tail him myself. IA's not to be trusted. They wouldn't have told us that Juan was in danger if we hadn't threatened them. The bastards."

Juan wasn't going to get back to sleep. He wasn't that naïve that he couldn't understand the significance of the phone call. He thought Morrison was a little off when they talked, but he never suspected that he was one of the bad guys. Collins and Littlefield were warning him to watch out for and stay away from Morrison. Juan noticed something else during the phone call. When the detectives heard that he and Morrison were together, their tone changed. It got lower with more emotion. Juan recognized the emotion. It was anger.

Anwar was in Omar's office when the first live TV News reports came in. They had been waiting to hear the details. Omar had not received word from the militia deliverymen, which he took as a sign that the arms exchange had been unsuccessful. "Turn the volume up." Anwar found the remote and pressed the volume button.

"...on scene at what appears to have been a shootout between officers of the ATF and a group of armed men. We haven't been allowed to speak to any of the government people, but we have seen at least seven bodies being removed from this warehouse located at 24th and Barber Streets in the warehouse district. Witnesses have reported hearing dozens of shots fired. Fortunately, none of the government agents were killed, but two had minor injuries. We'll have more for you as the story develops. Live at the scene of a mid-morning shootout, this is Gwen King, WRHT News."

"So far, so good." Omar wanted to hear word that the government had discovered a nuclear device in the warehouse. But he realized that the government would never release that information to the public. And it was possible that the Russians had not yet delivered the bomb. He would probably never know what happened to it.

The phone rang and Omar picked it up. "Hello..." He realized that he was on his cell phone and he caught himself. He had almost announced the name of the auto body shop.

"Omar, this is Morrison."

"Yes, Morrison, what is it?"

"They're on to me. I don't know how, but they must have seen me tracking the janitor kid."

"What? Damn-it, I told you to keep your mouth shut and back off. Didn't I?"

"Yeah but..."

"Yeah but nothing. You're going to screw up and get yourself caught. Do they know anything?"

"No, not that I can tell."

"Then they're speculating and they're trying to rattle you. Stay calm and keep your mouth shut. Let me lay it out for you. You are the only one who knows about me. You are the only one who knows my name. You are my only loose end. Do you understand what I'm saying?"

"Yes."

"You're a cop. Try and act like one." Omar signed off. He looked at Anwar. "This guy is a fucking liability. I can't ignore him much longer. Put someone on him. If I decide he has to go, I want it done quickly."

CHAPTER THIRTY-SEVEN

Collins and Littlefield started the daily morning meeting at 1:00 pm. They updated everyone with all the information they had, including Morrison's involvement with the case. They cautioned the team about leaking information especially since one of their own was playing a role.

"If any information gets out to the press or anyone outside this room, you'll have hell to pay."

The troops around the conference table were shaking their heads in disbelief. "I've worked with Morrison. He's been a straight arrow for as long as I've known him." One of them said. "What proof do you have that Morrison's dirty? The word of IA, come on…"

"You're right; everything we've got is word of mouth from IA. It's time we did some old fashioned police work. IA said that there was a liquor store robbery. Let's prove it." Collins handed out assignments to check out the liquor store with a forensic team. Team members were also assigned to find the owners of the store and to look into their financials. The security tape from the mall across the street from the store was to be confiscated. The store clerks were to be interviewed or interrogated depending on how cooperative they were.

"Omar has or had a connection with that liquor store. We're going to find it and we're going to find him. Everyone get to work."

The team filed out of the conference room. Littlefield nt to his desk and turned it so he would have an structed view of Morrison. He made sure everyone saw him do it.

Morrison, sitting at his desk, saw the glances he was getting from the team. He opened his desk drawer and looked at his throw away thirty-eight. *"It wouldn't be the worst way to go,"* he thought to himself. *"At least I'd get to take some of these assholes with me."* He closed his drawer and leaned back in his chair. *"Everything is circumstantial. They have nothing."* Morrison had a new mantra. He repeated it and it calmed him.

Morrison knew he was finished. Even if his current troubles went away, no one on the force would ever trust him again. Omar was not going to be any help; in fact, Omar was more of a threat than a friend. He decided to hold on for a couple of months, then retire. But first he needed to take out some insurance in case Omar decided to move on him.

After work, Morrison planned to go to his bank and write down everything he knew about Omar and his operation. There were a number of facts that Morrison managed to accumulate that would easily put Omar away and destroy everything he built. Of course he'd add his belief that Anwar and Hassan had killed Donovan and Adams. He'd write it all down and put it in his safety deposit box. Then he planned to stop by the Law Offices of Haden and Winston to give his attorney, Ben Springer, a letter to be opened in the event of his death.

Once Morrison was sure he had enough insurance to get him to retirement and beyond, then he'd take Omar's advice. He'd act like a cop.

CHAPTER THIRTY-EIGHT

Sanders was watching both his computer monitor and the office TV. The reports confirmed that there were eight people killed in the ATF raid, one inside the warehouse and the other seven out in front. No agents were killed, but two had minor injuries. Four of the dead were of Middle Eastern descent and the other four were Caucasian. One of the dead was shot with a .45-caliber bullet and the other seven were shot with .308 Winchester rounds. The .308 rounds were obviously fired from a sniper rifle.

The ATF snipers had discharged their weapons, but they said they shot away from the warehouse at another sniper on an office rooftop. Ballistics would have to verify that the ATF snipers didn't fire the kill shots.

According to the agent in charge, the raid wasn't a complete failure. They had two individuals in custody and they confiscated a number of illegal firearms. No theories were offered as to who did the killing. The local authorities had been brought in to lock down the area. The office building used by the sniper was searched from top to bottom. No one saw anything.

Omar kept the TV in the office on to get the updates of the ATF raid. The news reporters were referring to the shooting as a massacre. The ATF spokesman was forced to say that the dead men were not killed by the ATF agents. But he wouldn't go into the details of the shooting. As far as

Omar was concerned, the details were obvious. Anwar had taken steps to ensure that the terrorists wouldn't survive the raid. Omar realized that Anwar's plan worked out well, but he was torn between punishing him for his boldness and rewarding him for his initiative. He decided that it would be best to do nothing.

Morrison finished his business at the bank and went back to the station to keep track of the progress on the case. He also had his day job to worry about, a jewelry store robbery. The robbery looked like a couple of amateurs pulled it off. In and out in six minutes. The customers and employees were forced to the floor. Jewelry cases were smashed, and rings and necklaces, not the best quality merchandise, were taken.

In the morning he and Detective Howard would interview the customers and employees, get a description of the stolen jewelry circulated and start visiting pawnshops and known fences. Tonight, he was going to sit at his desk, pretend to plan his case activities and watch Collins and Littlefield do their thing.

When Morrison entered the squad room, only Collins and a few other team members were there. Littlefield came in two minutes later. Morrison smiled when he made the connection between his movements and Littlefield's. The activity in the conference room was winding down and people were leaving for the evening. Morrison walked past the conference room on the way to the men's room and he heard someone say, "Meet you at the liquor store in the morning..."

Morrison wondered how they made that connection.

Back at his desk, Morrison thought he should call Omar and calmly tell him about the liquor store reference. Now that he knew he had a tail, he was going to be extra careful. He rocked back and forth in his chair. He figured that Collins and Littlefield weren't leaving until he left. He thought about staying all night just to piss them off. He suddenly stiffened, *"Son of a bitch. If they're tailing me, they probably have a tap on my phones too!"* Morrison turned red. *"Christ! What did I say on those calls to Omar?"* He got up and rushed out of the squad room.

When Juan showed up for work, Littlefield was there, sitting in the conference room. "Were you waiting for me?" Juan asked.

"No, I was working and lost track of time. How are you doing?"

"I'm okay. I was a little shook up after your call this afternoon."

"Relax, there's nothing to worry about. We've got your back."

"What does that mean? I was here by myself with one of the bad guys who's involved in a double homicide, and you've got my back!"

"I've already talked to Morrison; he's no threat to you. He won't be bothering you anymore."

"How long have you guys known that Morrison was mixed up in this?"

"A few days."

"Why didn't you tell me?"

"We didn't think you needed to know. You were only supposed to be dealing with the facts of the case."

"Isn't Morrison one of the facts of the case? You guys are playing games with me, aren't you?"

"No, Juan, it's not like that. We had no idea that Morrison would figure out that you were helping us."

"If you guys want my help, you'd better not hold out on me again. Fifty bucks a week is not worth risking my life for."

"Okay Juan, it won't happen again." After apologizing twice, Littlefield filled Juan in on the latest facts of the case and the plan to fully investigate the liquor store robbery and the people working there.

Juan said that he thought there was more to the robbery than he first believed. He knew that someone had gotten hurt, but he also thought that the killings were more than just revenge. Now he had the idea that the robbers were killed to shut them up. He thought that they had stolen information about a crime being planned. Something Big.

"The murders were a little extreme as payback for a robbery," Littlefield said in agreement. "They could have just been beaten and let go. They couldn't go to the police and complain; they were thieves. You might be on to something. I'll check the NCIC data base to see if there were any major crimes that happened since the time of the murders." Littlefield left the room and went to his desk. He signed on to his computer and began querying the database.

After a half hour, he signed off the computer and slumped in his chair. Juan had just finished his work in the restrooms and he saw Littlefield motioning for him to come over.

"The biggest thing that happened recently was an ATF raid on an arms sale about twenty-five miles south of here. Eight people were shot and killed, Mid-Eastern and Mid-Western types, and a small weapons cache was seized. A curious thing was that the ATF didn't kill anybody. A non-ATF sniper killed seven of them. I don't know if this ties in with our case, but it's big and it's strange."

"If advance information about that gun sale was stolen, I could understand why they wanted it back; and why they'd kill anyone who knew about it." Juan paused and said, "Speaking of advance information, does the report say how the ATF found out about the gun sale?"

"No it doesn't. That's a very good question. But it's a question that can wait until tomorrow to be answered. I'm going home and get some sleep. You keep in touch." Littlefield gathered his things as Juan went back to work. He waved at Juan as he entered the elevator. "Take it easy, kid."

"Okay, goodnight.

CHAPTER THIRTY-NINE

After Morrison left the station house, his first stop was to get a pre-paid cell phone. He couldn't believe that he hadn't thought that they had tapped his phones. He tried to think. *"How long have they been on to me?"* He remembered two calls to Omar since the interview with Collins and Littlefield. *"What did I say? What did I say?"* He knew that whatever else happened, he couldn't tell Omar that his conversations had been monitored. He had to prove to Omar that he was an asset. He was already on thin ice.

He called Omar. The phone rang five times. "Hello, who is this?"

"Omar, it's me."

"Caller ID said 'no data' I almost didn't pick up the call."

"I got a new phone just to be careful. This is me acting like a cop."

"Good idea. What have you got for me?"

"Somehow, they found out about the liquor store robbery. You need to sever all connections with the store."

"Not a problem, the store's not in my name. It's owned by a holding company, but it's in the Salims' name. The Salims, the couple who are running it now, have never met me. They have seen some of my people, but they really only knew Azlan and he's gone."

"Be absolutely sure they can't connect you with the

store."

"I am. I only went there on Saturdays for a few hours. It's a miracle that I was the one who found Azlan. Wait, I did call Azlan's girlfriend to tell her that he left town."

"Did you use your name?"

"I may have."

"Then she may have to have an accident."

"That sounds a little drastic. One phone call made weeks ago. She's probably forgotten about it by now."

"Let's run it down. The old couple at the store knew Azlan, Azlan went missing, Azlan's girl filed a missing person report, the girl gets an interview with the cops about her missing boyfriend, the girl recalls a phone call from a man from the liquor store. If you mentioned your name, I think she'll probably remember it. Better safe than sorry."

"Okay, you've made your point. Have you got anything else for me?"

"No, that's it."

"Thanks for the call."

"My pleasure." Morrison was glad he made the call. It went better than he expected. He had proved his value and he planned to continue to do so.

Collins decided to call John Smith before the morning team meeting in case IA had discovered anything new. Collins thought that Morrison looked agitated when he left work and maybe he called the mysterious Omar. Collins made the call.

"Good morning, this is John Smith, Internal Affairs."

"This is Collins and Littlefield, you seem cheerful this morning. Do you have anything new on my case?"

"No, but I've got some bad news concerning my case, the one against Ken Morrison, dirty cop. Last night after work, Morrison went to the Phone Shop on 15th street. According to the clerk there, he purchased a pre-paid cell phone."

"Shit! I guess that's the end of that source of intel."

"Another thing, my man spotted Littlefield tailing Morrison for a while yesterday. He needs to cut it out. He's not good at it and Morrison knows him. Let's not step on each other's toes."

"Littlefield did that because you failed to tell us that Morrison had some crazy idea about the janitor kid and might have tried to hurt him."

"It's not true is it? You don't have the kid working for you, do you?"

"Of course not! He's just a good kid, like a squad mascot. We like him and you guys weren't going to do anything to stop Morrison."

"Point taken. It would have made life a little easier if Morrison had moved on the kid and we took him down for it."

"Forget easy and remember 'Protect and Serve'."

"Okay, I hear you."

"One question before you go," Littlefield said. "Do you have any contacts with the ATF?"

"Not directly, but I know someone who knows

someone. Why do you ask?"

"I'd like to know where ATF got the tip about the arms sale down south. We think it might be related to our case, loosely related."

"I'll make a call. You guys take care." Smith signed off the call.

Collins hung up and began to gather the troops for the morning meeting. The normal enthusiasm exhibited by the team was missing. The knowledge that solving the case also meant that one of their own would be brought down put a damper on things. Collins ignored the team's mood. "We lost the phone tap. Our guy figured out that there was a tap on his phones and he bought a pre-paid cell phone."

The expressions around the table looked more like relief than disappointment. Now Morrison would stop directly incriminating himself. "He is still being tailed. What else is going on?" Collins pointed at an officer standing in the corner.

"The forensic team at the liquor store is still gathering evidence. So far, they sprayed luminol around the store and despite a crude cleaning effort, a large area of blood splatter was found. Forensics is hoping to find good blood and DNA samples in the store."

"That's evidence of some violence, but not of a robbery. Anything else?"

"A .22 caliber shell casing was found under a display shelf."

"Any luck on the owner and the financials?"

"Not yet. That's going to take some time to figure out. We're working on it."

"Keep at it. We've got a new theory that Donovan and Adams were killed because they stole information about a crime that had not yet been committed. The thought is that they were tortured to retrieve the information and killed to shut them up. Think about it while you're working on your assignments. The old couple who are running the store are scheduled to come to the station for an interview at 1:00 pm. Those of you interested in seeing the interview, be in the observation room at that time."

The daily call between Sanders and IA was cordial. Neither side thought that they had anything to offer. "How'd that ATF raid turn out? Any word on who killed those guys and why?"

"No, the word is that they're still investigating, which means that they have no idea. What's new on your case?" asked Sanders.

"You mean cases. Morrison is still making contact with Omar in the dirty cop case. Unfortunately he figured out that his phones were being tapped and he got a new phone. In the double homicide case, my informant tells me that the team is going over the liquor store with a fine-tooth comb to verify that there was a robbery. They are going to interview the store clerks. Their latest theory is that the homicides were done to shut the victims up about information of a crime that was about to be committed. Can you follow all that?"

"Yes, and it makes sense. It always bothered me that the murders were, excuse the pun, overkill. A good beating and a threat of death would have worked just as well if they just wanted to retaliate for the theft. But, if they had to make sure their secret was kept safe, homicide was their only option."

"Okay, if you can follow that, the current thinking is that the crime covered up was the ATF arms sale. Now the cops want to know where the ATF got its tip that there was going to be a sale. Do you know anyone over there?"

The mention of the possible ATF arms sale connection caused Sanders to perk up. "Yeah, I know people, but it's a waste of time to ask. The standard answer, if there is one, is a confidential informant. They'll never say anything beyond that."

"Okay, if the theory holds and the arms sale is the crime, Omar is a major player and someone you Feds want to meet."

"Absolutely," said Sanders.

"Good. It occurs to me that you haven't contributed that much to this investigation. Now maybe you'll add some resources, use some government technology, do some shit and help find this Omar character."

"I'll see what I can do. Talk to you later." Sanders ended the call.

CHAPTER FORTY

Omar wasn't comfortable with the idea of getting rid of Azlan's girlfriend, Bonnie. *"What good would it do?"* He thought to himself. *"Maybe I mentioned my name and maybe she remembers it, maybe not."* He mulled it over for a few minutes then he called Hassan.

"Hello."

"Hassan, Azlan had a girlfriend by the name of Bonnie Rupp. Have you ever met her?"

"No, Omar."

"She may be a problem for us. You have to get rid of her."

"Where can I find her?"

"She's the manager at the Three Flames restaurant. Watch her for a day or two and learn her routine. Take her out and make it look like an accident."

"It will be done."

Omar hung up still feeling unsure about his decision. He knew that however you looked at the problem, Morrison was still the only direct link between him and the murders. Azlan's girl wasn't the real threat. He had a few days to call off Hassan, if he changed his mind.

Morrison and his partner were doing their day job,

investigating the jewelry store robbery. Morrison was just going through the motions. His mind was elsewhere. They made the rounds of the local pawnshops to alert them to look out for the stolen pieces. They decided to stop for lunch before going back to the station.

Morrison pulled into the Sandwich Shop parking lot and found a place close to the building. As he and Howard went in the store, he noticed a dark sedan, a typical Government Issue vehicle, pull into the lot and park in the spot furthest from the door.

They sat at a table near the window and looked over the menus. Their waitress, Wendi, came and took their order. Morrison ordered a meatball sandwich and Howard ordered a salad. Morrison looked out into the parking lot; the sedan was still there. He also noticed a black SUV at the other end of the lot. He could make out that there were drivers in both cars, but neither of them came into the store for lunch. He wasn't sure whether or not the SUV was there before he arrived. But he was sure the sedan driver was tailing him.

They finished their lunches and were heading back to the station. Howard, as always, wanted to make a quick stop. This time it was at the dry cleaners on South Olive Avenue. She said it would save her from having to come back to this part of town after work. Morrison agreed and was able to find a spot right in front of the store. Howard hopped out and went inside. Morrison looked into the rear view mirror to see if the sedan was still following him. There it was, a block behind, parked in a bus stop.

Dry cleaning safely in hand, they made it back to the station. Howard went to her car to put the dry cleaning in her trunk and Morrison headed inside. As he turned to watch Howard walk away, he saw a black SUV turn the corner and drive past the station. He thought for a moment, and then he said, "*Omar.*"

In the station, the interview with the old couple from the liquor store was underway. The interview with the Salims did not yield much. They said that they were working toward ownership of the store; a management company in New York currently owned it.

They did mention that one of their workers left suddenly, causing them to scramble to find a suitable replacement. The worker who left was Azlan Yardim. They said that Azlan was a good worker and he did all the hiring and firing. When he left, the people he hired began to leave too. They were asked if Omar worked in the store. They didn't react when they heard the name.

Collins and Littlefield weren't buying the old couple's story, but they couldn't get them to change it. The interview lasted over an hour. Collins sensed that the couple had had enough and were about to lawyer up, so he ended it and let them go.

They were no help, but he searched the NCIC database for Azlan Yardim anyway. The data base search yielded the missing persons report filed by Bonnie Rupp. He saw the request that the FBI be notified and he planned to do it later. The missing persons report had as much information on Bonnie Rupp as it did on Azlan Yardim. Collins called Ms. Rupp at her home and got no answer. He called her at her work, the restaurant, and was put on hold. After five minutes, the call was picked up. "Hello."

"Hello, Ms. Rupp. This is Detective Don Collins. I'm calling in reference to the missing person report you filed."

"Have you found Azlan? Is he all right?"

"No, he hasn't been found. I'm hoping you could come to the station to discuss Mr. Yardim. It would help our investigation."

"I don't know what more I could tell you. I told the other officer everything I knew when I filled out the report."

"It would be a big help. Could you come to the station now?"

"There's no way I could do it now. We've got to deal with the lunch cleanup, and then we'll have to set up for dinner. I could be there around four."

"Okay, that'll be fine. Thank you."

"Goodbye." Bonnie was becoming annoyed. The police didn't seem concerned when she filled out the report. Now they wanted her back.

Collins wasn't sure what help Bonnie Rupp could be, but he wanted to find out as much as he could about Azlan Yardim.

Morrison came in the squad room and sat down at his desk. He was getting used to the stares and glares he got from his co-workers. He went over the notes from his case and the list of stolen jewelry and he re-read the storeowner and witness statements. He looked up occasionally to see the activity in the conference room.

He saw the old couple being escorted out of the squad room. The old man stopped in the men's room while his wife waited for him in the hall. Morrison got up and took the elevator down to the lobby. He waited for a few minutes and exited the building with the Salims. "I want to thank you again for coming in to talk with us." Morrison said.

"It was a waste of time. We've got a business to run.

That other detective was rude to us, asking us a bunch of stupid questions." The old man was livid.

"I'm sorry, I'm sure he didn't mean to be rude."

"Asking us about our employees, he acted like we didn't know what we were doing. He even asked us about people we never even heard of. Who the hell is Omar anyway?"

Morrison thought he'd been hit with a brick. "Once again, I'm sorry for the inconvenience."

"We just want to get the hell out of here!" With that the old people got in their car and drove off.

"They already have his name. How did they get his name?" Morrison stood there in the parking lot stunned. *"It's all right. It's all right. What can they do with it? Unless Omar's been stupid or careless, having his first name is worthless."* Morrison walked around the parking lot to clear his head.

Morrison pulled out his cell phone and called Omar.

"What have you got?"

"I can't figure out what's going on. They've talked to the old couple from the store and they got nothing. But the old guy told me that they asked him if he knew Omar."

"What?"

"I don't know how they got your name. But they got it."

"What else do they know?" asked Omar.

"They know that Azlan worked at the store and I heard that they had a forensic team look over the place. The important thing is that nothing they got leads them to you."

"That's right," said Omar. "The only connection I have

with this case is you."

"Let's talk about that." Morrison clenched his jaw. "I spotted a black SUV following me this afternoon. You wouldn't know anything about that would you?"

"No, of course not."

"That's good because I took out a little insurance. I wrote down everything I know about your operation, and put it in a safe place. If anything happens to me, my information on you will go where it will do the most good. Do you understand?"

"That's not necessary. There's no need for threats."

"I'm just telling you how things are. I don't expect to see that SUV again. And if it's not too late, you can call off the hit on Azlan's girlfriend since they already know your name. I'll keep in touch." Morrison hung up.

Bonnie hoped to run over to the Police Station and get back to the restaurant before the dinner rush. She grabbed her things and headed out. The station was only five blocks away, so she decided to walk. It was still warm, but it was nothing like the afternoon heat three hours ago. It was ten minutes to four so there was no need to hurry. She wasn't anxious to talk to the cops anyway.

Hassan had seen Bonnie leave the restaurant. He knew her work hours, but he hadn't had time to observe any pattern to her movements. She didn't go to her car. He guessed that she was going shopping before the dinner shift. He thought to himself that an accident was an accident. If it happened after careful study of the victim's comings and goings or it happened right away, what difference would it make?

She walked at a leisurely pace, and she wasn't looking in the shop windows as she passed them. He suspected that she was going somewhere specific and she had an appointment at the top of the hour. He assumed that she wouldn't have enough time for a doctor or dentist appointment. Even a hair appointment wouldn't allow her to get back to work in time. He remembered that the police station was nearby.

He stopped tailing her and drove the remaining three blocks to the station and parked on the street. She would have to pass by him if she were heading here. Preventing her from talking to the cops was enough justification to speed up his timetable. He waited. If she was coming here, she'd have to cross the street right in front of him. Hassan smiled and thought to himself that it was up to her if she was going to live to see another day.

A minute later, he saw her in the rearview mirror. She would have to pass by his car and cross the street to get to the station. As she crossed, he would pull out and hit her from behind. She wouldn't have a chance. She approached the car. She passed by. As she stepped out in the street between the parked cars a half a block in front of him, Hassan's phone rang. He ignored the phone, and pulled out into the street. He'd time it so that she'd walk right into the speeding car. The phone kept ringing. Just as he was on top of her, he gunned the engine. When she heard the sound of the engine, she lunged backward into the space between the cars and Hassan sped past.

Hassan was astounded. He couldn't understand how she did it. In the rearview mirror, he could see her leg sticking out between the parked cars. She had fallen to the ground and couldn't have been able to see him or his car. He quickly turned the corner and kept driving. The phone was still ringing. He picked up the call.

"Hassan, this is Omar. Forget about the girl. She can't hurt us after all."

"Are you sure, Sir? She's talking to the cops now."

"It's all right. She doesn't know anything. Leave her alone."

"Yes, Sir. I will." Hassan signed off and grunted his disapproval.

CHAPTER FORTY-ONE

Bonnie entered the police station looking over her shoulder at the people on the street. She asked for Collins at the receptionist's desk and was given a badge and directed to the second floor squad room. Having been alerted to her arrival, Collins greeted Bonnie at the elevator. He saw that she was disheveled and the sleeve of her dress was dirty. "Ms. Rupp, are you all right?"

"Someone tried to kill me just now out front."

"What happened?"

"I was crossing the street in front of the building and a car came up behind me and tried to run me over. I dove back the way I came and the car accelerated on by. I've never been so scared."

"Did you see who was driving and the make and model of the car?"

"I didn't get a chance to see anything. It happened so fast. But the way it just missed me and kept on going, I knew he was trying to kill me."

Collins walked her to his desk and had her sit down in a guest chair. "Try to calm down; I'll get you some water." He left her for a minute, made a call and came back with the water.

"Aren't you going to do something?"

"I've called downstairs for officers to canvas the area to see if anyone saw anything. Hopefully, we'll find a witness.

But without a description of the suspect or the car, there's nothing I can do. Do you know of any reason someone would have to hurt you?"

"No, I haven't done anything to anybody. I'm not seeing anyone. No one has a reason to hurt me. The only interesting thing I've done in the last month was to file a missing person report."

"Let's have a talk about that. Just relax for a minute and catch your breath."

"I'm fine."

"I need you to tell me everything you can. Were you involved with Azlan Yardim?"

"Yes."

"How long had you been seeing him?"

"We were together about two and a half months. What's this all about? Was Azlan in some kind of trouble? Is that why he left town so abruptly?"

"What we've been able to find out so far is that Mr. Yardim was in this country on an expired visa and his disappearance is suspicious. Now let's continue. How did you meet Mr. Yardim?"

The interview lasted twenty minutes. Bonnie didn't have much to say. She said that she and Yardim weren't really serious but he just disappeared without a word. She said that she got a call from a man who said that he was Yardim's boss and that Azlan was leaving town and wasn't expected to return. She also said that after he disappeared, a man from the FBI came to the restaurant and questioned her. Bonnie voiced her concerns to him that Yardim would never have left town without seeing her and saying goodbye. Collins asked her the FBI agent's name and she remembered that his last name was Sanders.

Collins arranged to have a patrolman drive her back to work. He gave her his card and promised to have cars drive by the restaurant and her residence at regular intervals. Collins found Littlefield at his desk. "Ms. Rupp, the woman who filed the missing person report, is convinced that somebody tried to kill her as she was coming in the station."

"What?"

"Yeah. She said a car was trying to run her down and she jumped out of the way. She didn't see the guy or the car; I've got patrolmen out looking for witnesses."

"Someone must have thought that she had something to tell us. Did she?"

"Yes, in a way. Guess who else has taken a part in our case?"

"Who's that?"

"The FBI. An agent named Sanders questioned Rupp after Azlan Yardim's disappearance."

"Knowing those assholes, they don't show up, ask questions and fade away. He's probably been shadowing us all along."

"I'll bet you're right. If the bureau has an interest in Yardim, they have an interest in Omar."

"This is getting crazy. The FBI wants Yardim and Omar, IA wants Morrison and we want Donovan's and Adams' killer, who we think is Omar; and it's all the same case." Littlefield scratched his head looking confused. "Why hasn't the FBI come forward and played an active role in the case?"

"Who knows? It's too late to get any answers. Let's call it a day."

"Fine with me. I think you should call the kid tonight and fill him in."

"I'll do that. I'd like to get his take on all of this."

On the way home, Collins stopped at the market and bought a steak, a bag of salad and a bottle of Merlot. Even in the ten items or less line, the bill came to $36.75. He was tempted to pull his gun and walk out of the store with his groceries. He didn't. He paid, walked to the parking lot, got in his car and drove home.

His apartment was Spartan, as one would expect. Divorced with no kids, he brought none of his past life to his new place. He had a big screen TV with cable and a DVR. His bed was large and comfortable. His neighbors knew he carried a gun so no one bothered him. Life was good.

He put the food away, grabbed a beer and plopped down in front of the tube. After a couple of news shows, the stories started to run together with a single recurring theme, "things are bad and getting worse".

He enjoyed cooking, but he didn't feel like being bothered with a big production today, so he had bought the steak. He cooked it, shook out half a bag of salad, re-heated some dinner rolls and opened the wine. He ate in front of the TV on a tray that rolled up close to the couch and covered his lap.

He watched four mind-numbing sitcoms and the late news before he cleared his tray and called Juan.

"Hello."

"Hi kid, how's it going?"

"Everything is fine, no problems. Are there any new developments with the case?"

Collins went over the events of the day, including the interviews with the old couple and Bonnie Rupp. He went over the encounter with Rupp in detail.

"If there was an attempt on her life, maybe the bad guys thought that Yardim told her something in a moment of intimacy."

"Calm down, kid. Suppress those hormones and exercise the gray matter."

"Okay," said Juan, a little embarrassed. "The man who called her to say that Yardim left town, could that have been Omar?"

"That's possible, but it isn't a good enough reason for attempted murder."

"They're working with imperfect information, just like we are."

"That's a good point, kid. They don't really know what she knows. What's your take on the FBI involvement?"

"That's a surprise. But, since they questioned Ms. Rupp, they must have been after Yardim for a federal matter."

"Yeah, an expired visa."

"Would an FBI agent be called in on an expired visa? Wouldn't that be someone from immigration?"

"You would think so, but after 9/11, who knows?"

"I think there are too many entities involved for us not to be stepping on each other's toes. We bumped into Internal Affairs working this case. I'll bet that the FBI bumped into them too. You are working with IA. Would they have told you if they were working with the FBI too?"

"No, they wouldn't," Collins said without hesitation.

"Jesus! Aren't we all on the same side?"

"Sometimes I'm not sure, kid."

"Organizational politics is too complicated for me. I guess that's a college course I haven't had yet. Getting back to the case, Omar wants to kill Ms. Rupp and Morrison, right?"

"Yeah."

"There was an attempt on Ms. Rupp. Suppose there's an attempt on Morrison? Isn't he the real threat to Omar?"

"That's good, kid. If Morrison thinks Omar is trying to kill him, he'll give him up. I love it."

"Detective, I know how you feel about Morrison. There only needs to be an attempt. The operative word is ATTEMPT."

Collins laughed, "Of course, kid, an attempt."

"I've got to get back to work. Goodnight, Detective."

"Goodnight, kid. You're worth every penny."

CHAPTER FORTY-TWO

Collins was in good spirits when he went into work in the morning. He caught himself whistling at his desk and he stopped before he disturbed anyone. He couldn't wait for Littlefield to come in so he could bounce Juan's idea off him.

Collins tried to come up with a plan to go after Morrison. He wondered, *"How does one attempt to murder a man who carries a gun without getting killed in the process?"* The attacker had to be careful not to be seen. It wasn't going to be as easy as he thought.

Littlefield walked in and headed for the coffee. Collins gave him a few minutes to get to his desk and settle in. Collins walked over to him. "I called the kid last night and he came through again."

"What did he say?"

"He said that chances are that the FBI guy and IA have probably been working together behind our backs. Those weren't his exact words, but it conveys the point. On our next call to Internal Affairs, which will be in about a half an hour, we'll ask them."

"Okay, anything else?"

"Yeah, he said we should make Morrison believe that Omar is trying to kill him."

"What? The kid said that?"

"Yes and it's a good idea. If Morrison thinks Omar is trying to take him out, he'll turn on Omar and give him up."

"Wait a minute; I can see a lot of problems. For one, the guy can shoot back at whoever shoots at him. And he won't be trying to miss. Another thing is the guy has a tail on him. Are you going to bring IA in on this little plan of ours?"

Collins thought for a moment and said, "No, we can't do that. Do you think we should forget about it?"

"No, I'm not saying it can't be done. But it's got to be done right."

"I know. This idea makes sense. I think we've got to try it. We're dead in the water otherwise. We've got to do something to jump start this case."

"Let's not rush into this. Let's take it slow and do our homework," said Littlefield with a thoughtful expression.

"Agreed. We'll figure out his routine, see if we can spot his tail and find out if it's even possible to get him."

"All right, let's do that. But first, let's see if we can take a short cut."

"What short cut?"

"He's already been tailed for weeks. Someone in IA already knows his routine. Let's ask them for it."

"Yeah, that's smart." Littlefield picked up the phone and made the call.

"Smith, Internal Affairs."

"Not so chipper this morning, huh? This is Littlefield and Collins."

"What do you guys want?"

"Just a friendly chat. First of all, we understand you've been working on our case with an agent Sanders of the FBI."

"How did you...? What makes you think that we were working with the FBI?"

"I thought so. Let's cut the crap. I know you've got too much integrity to tell us what you've been doing with Sanders." Collins almost choked on his words. "I just want you to arrange an introduction."

"Why don't you go to the bureau directly?"

"Those assholes probably wouldn't admit that Agent Sanders even exists. Why don't you arrange a three way call and we can all work together?"

"I'll see what I can do."

"This is Littlefield; I understand that you want me to stop tailing Morrison. Is that right?"

"Yeah, you don't know what you're doing and you're making our job harder."

"Sorry about that. But we've got a murder case to solve and I've got to gather information on Morrison's movements."

"That job is already being done."

"That may be true, but we're not getting any benefit from your tailing Morrison. To get the information we want, we've going to have to follow him ourselves."

"What information do you want?"

"We want to know his routine, his comings and goings. You know, the usual."

"What if we give you a copy of the report we put together covering his movements?"

"That would work. That's a good idea. Why don't you have someone run a copy down to us?"

"Okay. Anything else?"

"No that's it. Good talking to ya." Littlefield hung up and chuckled. "Now that's done, let's get back to planning the hit."

CHAPTER FORTY-THREE

Even after a night's sleep, Bonnie was still shaken by the attempt on her life. She saw the patrol car cruise the neighborhood, but it was small comfort. She wanted the cops to do something, not just wait for the next attempt.

She remembered that the FBI agent had given her a card. He seemed like a nice man. He had a nice face and kind eyes. When she replayed their conversation in her mind, she got the impression that he was interested in what she said. No, he was interested in her. She didn't have a great deal of experience with men, but she had enough to know how to influence them. She didn't think she was good at it, but she had a great incentive. She would call him, play up to him, and then maybe he'd protect her.

She searched her purse for the card. She was afraid that she might have thrown it away. She found it. The kitchen phone was next to her and she reached for it. *"No, I'll use my cell phone."*

She reasoned that he had caller ID and she wanted him to have her cell phone number without having to give it to him directly. Her cell phone was in her bedroom on the nightstand. She went to the bedroom and sat on the bed. A smile formed on her lips. The idea of having an FBI agent for a boyfriend appealed to her. She picked up the phone and paused. *"Maybe I'm getting ahead of myself. Maybe I misread him. Oh, what the hell."* She made the call. She expected to be connected to an automated system and be passed around or put on hold.

"This is Agent Sanders. How can I help you?"

Getting directly connected threw her off guard. She quickly collected her thoughts. "Agent Sanders, this is Bonnie Rupp. I don't know if you remember me. We spoke a few weeks ago about the disappearance of a friend of mine, Azlan Yardim."

"Yes, Ms. Rupp, I do remember you. Have you thought of something else you need to tell me?" Sanders was delighted to get the call. He planned to look for any opportunity to turn the call into a meeting.

"Not exactly. I've got something to tell you, but it's kind of awkward over the phone."

"Maybe we can meet and talk."

"Yes, that will be great. How soon could you see me?"

"What time do you finish work, Ms. Rupp?"

"Not until late, after 10 pm. I don't want to wait that long. Are you free for lunch?"

"Yes, I could manage that."

"Why don't I buy you lunch? Meet me at my restaurant at 12:30."

"Wonderful... I mean fine. I'll see you then. Goodbye."

"Goodbye." Bonnie was beaming. "He said 'wonderful'. I didn't misread him."

Her mood turned serious in an instant. She had a lot to do before lunchtime. Besides having to work, she had to look like a million bucks. She didn't want to appear too easy or anxious. But she wanted to cultivate or activate his interest in her. And she wanted to move fast. She wanted a live-in bodyguard while her body was still alive.

Sanders was on cloud nine. Bonnie had been on his mind since they first met. He couldn't believe his luck. They were going to have lunch. What was he going to talk about? He remembered that she was interested in the case of the missing boyfriend, not in him. Before he could write 'Mrs. Bonnie Sanders' a thousand times in his notepad, he had better come up with something related to the case to impress her.

He looked at his notes. There wasn't much he could tell her. He could say that he suspected that Yardim met with foul play and it was likely that he wouldn't be coming back. He didn't want her to have any hope of being reunited with Yardim. He was a suspected bad guy. She shouldn't have anything to do with him anyway.

Sanders had to find a way to turn the conversation to a more personal nature. He could tell his life story in ten minutes flat. He'd told it before to women that interested him. Surprisingly, he didn't have much success with those other women. He decided it would be better if he got her to talk about herself. Women love that.

Collins got the report on Morrison's movements. It covered eighteen days. Morrison had no life at all according to what Collins read. He worked, went to the neighborhood bar, and went home. Occasionally he shopped for groceries.

Morrison didn't have much going for him, but as a target, he was perfect. He was predictable. They knew in advance where he was going and when he was going to be there.

Littlefield came up with the idea of a sniping incident. They could take a shot at him from a distance out of range of his handgun. Morrison's first reaction would be to take cover and before he gathered himself to return fire, the sniper would be gone. Even Morrison's tail wouldn't have time to react. It also helped that Littlefield was an ex-Marine who owned a suitable weapon.

The detectives skipped lunch to gather information to further their plan. They walked through Morrison's neighborhood to find the best spot to pull off their plan.

"What a shithole. I wouldn't walk around here after dark if I didn't have a gun."

"Yeah, but it's perfect for our purposes. There are plenty of abandoned buildings, few people around. It's got bars and crack houses, and no one would even notice the sound of gunfire. I love it," said Littlefield.

They had to make sure that the sniper had a way to exit the area without being seen. An abandoned apartment building a few blocks away from Morrison's bar looked like a good spot. It was three hundred yards away with a clear view of the front entrance. There were over a dozen windows in the building that were facing the bar. No one would even be able to tell where the shot came from.

Collins went back to the office to conduct the staff meeting, while Littlefield stayed and went through the building. The power was off, so he would have to have night vision goggles to make his way in and out of the building. The floors and stairs were still in good shape. He figured that after taking the shot and dismantling the rifle, he could be out of the building in two minutes.

He went through every room to verify that there were no squatters. He found a spot behind the building where he could park a car. He spent another hour in the building and walked through the neighborhood again. Satisfied that he'd done everything he needed to do, he went back to the office.

CHAPTER FORTY-FOUR

Sanders walked in the Three Flames Restaurant at 12:15 after having spent fifteen minutes sitting outside in his car. He stood by the 'Wait to be Seated' sign and looked around the floor. The place was busy. A hostess greeted him and before he could ask for Bonnie, he spotted her across the room heading toward him.

"You're early," she said as she smiled and took his hand. She was gorgeous. He remembered that she was attractive, but she had outdone herself.

"Traffic wasn't as bad as I expected."

"We have a room in the back," she said as she led him through the dining room to a hallway that led to the private rooms. "I hope you don't mind the separate room, but it's difficult to hear yourself think in the public area."

"I don't mind at all. You did say you wanted to talk."

The room looked like it could accommodate a party of ten. It was tastefully decorated. There were four separate tables, only one had place settings. They sat and a waiter appeared, coming through a door on the back wall. He poured water and gave them each a menu. "Do you like fish?" she asked.

"Yes, very much."

She turned to the waiter and said. "We'll have the snapper. And we don't want to be disturbed until our food is ready." She passed back the menus and the waiter left. "The snapper was flown in fresh this morning. I'm sure you'll enjoy it. I know how busy you must be and I don't want to waste your time."

Sensing her agitation, Sanders said, "Just relax, I don't consider being here a waste of time. Now tell me what's wrong."

"The police called me in to talk with them about the missing person report I filed. On the way to the station, I think someone tried to kill me."

"What! What happened?"

Bonnie could see the genuine concern in Sanders face. "As I was crossing the street going to the station, a car came from behind me and almost ran me down. I had to dive between two cars to avoid getting hit."

"Did you see who it was?"

"No."

"What about the make and model of the car, did you see it?"

"No." Bonnie sunk into her chair.

"Can you think of anyone who might want to cause you harm?"

"No. These are the same questions that the police asked me. They said that there is not much they can do. For now, they have patrol cars passing by the restaurant and my home. They want to catch the killer after he's done his job."

Bonnie's attempt at humor missed the mark with Sanders. "If there was anything I could do, I would."

"Do you know anything about Azlan that I should know about?" asked Bonnie.

"I don't think so. He was in this country on an expired

student visa and I don't think he's coming back. That's all I know. I'm sorry about your friend. I know that he must have been special to you."

"Apparently not," said Bonnie.

The food arrived and the conversation turned to the restaurant and Bonnie's job. She had worked her way up from hostess to manager. The hours were long and the work was demanding. She didn't have much time off, only Sundays, which she liked to spend at museums or art galleries. Sanders expressed an interest in art and Bonnie's mood changed.

She asked him about himself and he resisted giving her the ten-minute life story. He just hit the high points which included being unmarried and uninvolved. He suggested that if she had the time and the patience, he'd love a guided tour of a museum or art gallery. She cleverly changed the subject instead of jumping at the opportunity just presented to her. They talked more about food and cooking.

"Thank you for ordering the snapper. Working here must make it difficult to watch your weight."

"Is there something wrong with my weight?"

"Oh no, of course not. You look beautiful. I mean, your weight is fine."

Bonnie laughed for the first time and he even liked the way she laughed. "I'm sorry, Agent Sanders. I'm only playing with you."

"My name is Ron."

"Well, Ron, my name is Bonnie and I'm free this Sunday if you'd care to start your museum and art tour."

"I would. Thank you. The only thing I'd like more is if

it was the start of my series of tours."

Bonnie smiled. "If you give me your cell number, I'll call you later in the week with the details of our Sunday."

They finished their meal, sharing bits and pieces of their life histories with intermittent awkward pauses. He gave her his home number, cell number and email address. It was the best lunch of his life.

CHAPTER FORTY-FIVE

Omar had a problem. Its name was Morrison. Anwar met Omar in his office to discuss the problem. "So Morrison says he's taken out some insurance, do you believe him?"

"I believe he'll do anything to save his ass. What I've been doing since I talked to him is trying to figure out what he knows. The only place we had meetings was at the liquor store. He doesn't know where we are. But he does know about the drug connections we have. He can't lead them to us, but he could mess up our business."

"He's an arrogant pain in the ass. I'd love to take him out."

"I know, but we can't. Not just yet. I should have never threatened him; I should have just gotten rid of him. Warning him was a big mistake. Now we've got to continue to work together. I'm sure it won't be long now before he tries to get a big payday by putting the squeeze on us."

"Suppose he just disappears, no body, no proof of death. He's under pressure from his own people. Why wouldn't he just take off?" said Anwar.

"No one would believe that he gave up his precious pension and just took off. We've got to leave him alone for now."

The staff meeting was just a rehash of the information

everybody already knew. The theory that Azlan was hurt or killed in the robbery and Donovan and Adams were tortured and killed to retrieve some information about a future crime was sound, but the proof was non-existent. They were at a dead end. Collins and Littlefield tried to reassure the troops that something would break and they'd solve the case. But everyone thought they were dreaming.

Morrison could sense that the case was winding down. The body language of the team members as they left the staff meeting told the whole story. They were all deflated except for Littlefield and Collins. Morrison watched his two colleagues and they watched him. Their shitty grins annoyed Morrison, but he knew they had nothing and their little task force was about to end. It wouldn't be long now, a few weeks at the most. He couldn't wait to get everyone off his back. Miserable as it was, he wanted his life back.

Morrison spent almost an hour calculating his pension if he left at the end of the year, then if he left after twelve months, then eighteen months. Howard interrupted him to tell him that a pawnbroker called. "A guy tried to pawn a piece of jewelry from the robbery."

"Tried?"

"Yeah, the guy and the pawnbroker haggled over the price and the guy said he'd think about it and come back."

"Okay, let's go and get a description. Maybe we will close a case this year after all."

The pawnshop was almost fifteen minutes away from the station. Morrison drove. "We're not going to have to stop and buy groceries on the way back, are we?"

"No, I ran all my errands yesterday. You never used to mind my little side trips before."

"That was when we were sleeping together. Now things are different."

Howard smiled. "I thought you liked going shopping with me. But it was just the fringe benefits you were interested in."

"You better believe it. By the way, how are things at home these days? I'm always willing to help out a friend in need."

"Things are all right for now, but it's nice to know that you've got my back." They both laughed a good laugh. It had been weeks since Morrison had anything to laugh about. It felt good.

The pawnshop was a dump. Merchandise was everywhere. You had to turn sideways to get through the shop to get to the counter. "You're lucky we're cops instead of fire marshals."

"Yeah, I've heard it before. But my layout helps me, cause I only have to deal with one creep, I mean 'customer', at a time."

"What have you got, Sol?"

Sol Green was a short fat man with a neat, white beard and a good sense of humor. Sol had worked with the police many times before and he had a good eye for merchandise and people. "A guy comes in about 1:30 wearing a dark blue shirt and tan pants and sneakers. He was white, clean-shaven, no scars, with a chain tattoo on his forearm. He brought in a gold pin, a frog with ruby eyes. A pin like that was on your list, so I called."

"Did the guy say when he'd be back?"

"No, but when he left, he went across the street to the

hotel on the corner. What an idiot."

"Thanks, Sol."

They walked across the street to the hotel. They talked to the desk clerk and found the room number of the suspect. In spite of Howard's objections, Morrison called the station for an entry team. The team arrived in eighteen minutes. Twelve minutes later, two suspects were in custody and most of the stolen jewelry was recovered.

Later, back at the station, Howard was given congratulations and Morrison was acknowledged for being on scene. He didn't expect much more. All he wanted to do was get out of the station and head to his friendly neighborhood bar. According to the report from Internal Affairs, Morrison closed the bar almost every night.

Littlefield finished work and went home. On the way, he reviewed the plan again. At home, he had put together a bag with all his equipment. He had the goggles, gloves and rifle, a pad to kneel on, ear plugs and some reflective tape to mark the way out of the building. The bag weighed about thirty pounds. It was manageable.

He went to the kitchen and put a Hungry Man dinner in the oven, set the timer and turned it on. He grabbed a beer and turned on the news. After dinner, he set his alarm for midnight and went to bed. Stretched out on his twin bed, he wondered what the downside would be if he didn't miss. He smiled and drifted off to sleep.

It seemed to Littlefield that he had just blinked and the alarm went off. It was midnight. He didn't feel rested at all. He went to the bathroom and went through his regular morning ritual. The shower woke him up. A black tee shirt and a pair of dark jeans were draped across the back of a chair in the bedroom. He put them on and grabbed his bag. He checked the bag one last time. He locked up and left.

Collins called Juan to let him know what was going on.

"It's going down tonight. We'll know by morning if the plan worked."

"What will happen to Morrison?"

"If he comes clean and tells us everything he knows, he'll probably get a deal. He'll lose his pension and end up serving some time. Of course, it depends on what IA has on him. If they can prove that he knowingly fingered Donovan and Adams for a hit, Morrison will go away for a long time."

"It almost sounds like Morrison would be better off if he keeps his mouth shut; no matter what happens tonight."

"The only thing that's going to be on his mind is that Omar tried to kill him. He'll do anything to save his ass. Being in prison is better than being dead."

"What if Morrison doesn't do anything? He's been under a lot of pressure. Suppose he decides he's done for anyway and he wants to go out as a policeman with a clean record instead of a dirty cop?"

"I suppose that's possible. But I think he'll give up Omar and sing like a bird."

"I hope you're right. Is it too late to stop Detective Littlefield? I just thought of a worst-case scenario. Suppose Morrison doesn't turn on Omar, and just reports the shooting as an attempt on his life. An attempt on a policeman's life gets some serious attention. Everyone would investigate the shooting and they would pull out all the stops. If Detective Littlefield leaves any clues at all, they'll find them and arrest him."

"Just calm down. Littlefield knows what he's doing. Everything's going to be fine. Stop worrying." Collins was talking to himself as well as Juan. He hoped he was right.

Littlefield was in position. He had a clear view of the bar's entrance and there was a spotlight above the door that illuminated everything in the front of the bar. It was 1:45 am and the place closed down at two. Littlefield looked around. The streetlights and the moon combined to make everything outside visible and the lack of power in the building made everything inside invisible. On the way in, Littlefield placed pieces of the reflective tape on floors and walls leading to the stairwell and on the banisters leading down and out of the building. When he put on the goggles, the tape pointed the way out like the emergency lighting on a plane.

It was 1:54; he had his weapon trained on the door. It opened. An older gentleman staggered out and walked down the street. Littlefield put his finger back on the trigger guard and relaxed. He wasn't absolutely sure if Morrison was even in the bar. He'd find out in a minute. It dawned on him that he was enjoying this little adventure more than he should.

At 2:01, the door opened and Morrison stepped out into the street. He paused under the spotlight to light a cigarette. Littlefield held his breath and took aim. Suddenly, the light over the bar door went out. Morrison was in the shadows. A shot that was too wide wouldn't convince him that there was a serious attempt on his life. A kill shot wouldn't yield the desired result either. Littlefield waited. The light from a street lamp reflected off Morrison's glasses and Littlefield had his shot. He aimed at a point just to the left of Morrison's ear. He took the shot just as Morrison moved to his right to head home.

Littlefield didn't wait to see Morrison's reaction. He expertly dismantled the rifle, packed his bag and put on the goggles. He picked up his things and quickly left the building.

On the street, Morrison ducked and took cover behind a parked car. It was almost a minute before he looked up to see where the shot came from. He had his gun out, but in his condition he couldn't defend himself. He heard the shot, but it sounded like it came from a great distance.

No one stirred on the street. Gunshots weren't uncommon in the neighborhood. He started to call 911, but he thought better of it. He didn't want law enforcement to have the number of his clean phone. He didn't think they cared if he lived or died anyway. He lifted his head and looked around. He didn't see any movement on the street and there weren't any unusual sounds. It was as though nothing had happened. He got up slowly and walked home.

He discovered that being shot at has a sobering effect. By the time he reached his place, he was clearheaded and ready to fight back.

"That damn son of a bitch, Omar!" he yelled.

He thought about how he would bring his ass down. He would go to the bank first thing in the morning and get his papers and anonymously send them to one of the guys on the double murder task force. He'd include the picture of Omar he had taken with his cell phone and had printed. He realized that his evidence lacked the punch it would have if it were sent posthumously.

"Shit," he muttered. "This is no good. I've got to do something else." He stretched out on the bed to think and he fell asleep.

CHAPTER FORTY SIX

At 11:00 am exactly, Ron Sanders knocked on Bonnie Rupp's door, ready for his tour of the area's art galleries. He spent the last two days learning as much as he could about the art currently on display in the area, so as not to appear completely stupid.

Bonnie opened the door and stepped back to let him in. He saw her and froze. She was lovely. She wore a white skirt and a tangerine blouse. Her outfit was simple, but very attractive. Her hair was up and even with her casual outfit, she had a formal look. She smiled at his reaction. "Well, come in. On time as usual."

"I wasn't about to keep you waiting. It's good to see you. How have you been?"

"Already with the small talk. Just relax; we're going to have a good time." Bonnie laid out the plan for the afternoon which included brunch at the restaurant, a museum stop and a walk through two of Bonnie's favorite galleries. She was in complete control.

The weather was perfect, and the food was delicious. The two of them did have a good time. The museum wasn't as boring as it was when Sanders went there a month ago. He found Bonnie interesting and easy to talk to and the time went by quickly.

Sanders was interested in Bonnie before the date, but now he was hooked. She saw him looking at her whenever he could. She knew the date had worked in her favor. She wondered how a dinner and dancing date would work out for them.

He walked her to her door and was about to say goodnight when she asked him in. "I'm still afraid that someone is trying to kill me. Come in and make sure the apartment is safe."

"Sure." He remembered the reason she wanted him around. "I'll check the place out."

He went through every room and checked the windows and doors. "Everything looks okay. I'll say goodnight now."

"Wait a minute, not so fast. It's still early. Would you like to have dinner? I could put something together in a few minutes."

"No, that's okay. You're safe now. You don't need me anymore today."

Bonnie looked stunned. "I didn't agree to go out with you for protection. I thought we had a good time today. I thought you liked me."

"I didn't mean it that way. I'm sorry. I do like you."

"You think I'm using you. Don't you?"

"It had crossed my mind. You do seem a little too good to be true. I have to ask myself, why would a woman like you want to be with me?"

"It appears we have some self-esteem issues to deal with." Bonnie stepped in close and kissed him gently on the lips. "I like you, but if you believe that I only want you around for protection, you can leave."

Sanders held her and kissed her and she responded to him. She walked him to the couch and sat him down. "Dinner will be ready in thirty minutes," she said as she walked to the kitchen. A minute later, she came back. "Protection is only a fringe benefit. Besides, for that to work, you'd have to be with me all day and all night." She smiled and went back to the kitchen.

It was almost 7:00 pm when Morrison woke up. His head felt like it was full of sand that shifted its weight whenever he turned his neck. He sat on the side of the bed and tried to think. "Why would Omar try to kill me? I told him about my insurance. I don't understand." He staggered to the bathroom and splashed water on his face. "Could it be somebody else?" He sat on the toilet and relieved himself.

After making coffee, he found half a sandwich in the refrigerator. He ate it and washed it down with the coffee. He picked up the phone and said, "Let's see what Omar has to say."

The phone rang twice. "Hello, who is this?"

"Good evening, Omar. Don't you recognize the number yet? Or maybe you never expected to hear from me again."

"What are you talking about?"

"I'm talking about the attempt on my life one of your guys tried this morning."

"That's bullshit. None of my people tried to kill you."

"I warned you what would happen."

"I didn't do it I tell you! What happened?"

"As if you didn't know, someone tried to shoot me in front of my hangout. A rifle shot I think."

"In the first place, my people don't miss. And now that I know that you have protected yourself, it makes no sense for me to try to kill you. Someone else is after you, not us."

"I'm pissed, Omar, and somebody's going to pay. Are you sure that you've got control of your people? Maybe one of your guys is trying to impress the boss by showing a little initiative."

"No. My people do what I say and only what I say." Omar remembered Anwar's use of a sniper to cover the business with the ATF.

"You'd better be right. Regardless, I'm going to need a show of good faith from you. Just to let me know you care. Let's say twenty thousand ought to do it."

"Why should I have to pay anything?"

"I put my ass on the line for you, and it's about time that I got paid for it. I'm serious. This is not a negotiation."

Omar started to protest, but he knew it would only be a waste of time. "Okay, I'll arrange for the money. How do you want me to deliver it?

"I'll call you tomorrow with the details of where to drop it. One last thing, there is a snapshot of you in my insurance papers, that I took with my cell phone. Don't fuck with me." He signed off.

Morrison thought about what Omar had said; his people didn't miss. Even if he missed with the first bullet, why wasn't there a hundred more to finish the job? Maybe the job was finished. Maybe it wasn't a hit; it was a miss. The cops could have tried to set him up to panic and turn on Omar. "It was those bastards, Collins and Littlefield." He said it out loud, and he knew it was true.

Bonnie and Sanders ate in silence. She cooked a steak to perfection and added mixed vegetables and a baked potato. Sanders did everything he could to keep from staring at her and telling her how beautiful she was. "How's your steak?" she asked.

"It's fine."

"I'm sorry; I should have asked you how you wanted it before I cooked it."

"No, really. It's fine."

"Then what's bothering you? I've been on my best behavior all day."

"You've been great. So great in fact, that I keep forgetting why I'm here."

"That again. I'm going to slap the shit out of you. You're here because I like you and I want you here. What's the matter with you? I practically throw myself at you and you …"

"I'm sorry, it just seems too good to be true."

"It's not going to be true unless you get it together." She got up and started clearing away the dishes in the middle of the meal."

"Stop, I'm sorry. I'm crazy about you and I'm afraid of doing something stupid, like falling for you when you're not really interested in me."

She stopped and turned to look at him. "That's twice you've accused me of using you. I don't like it. You'd better learn how to trust me or we won't be together long."

"We're together?"

"Just barely." He quickly got up and took her in his arms. She resisted, but not too much. She turned away as he tried to kiss her. Then she turned back. He felt the moistness of her cheek. He pulled back and saw a tear.

"I'm sorry," he said and kissed her tenderly. They held each other for a long time. He felt himself growing involuntarily. Suddenly, she pushed away from him. He thought his erection repulsed her.

"What do you mean, you're crazy about me?"

"I thought it was obvious. You act surprised. I've done everything I could not to scare you off. I didn't stare at you and I wanted to all day. I was careful not to compliment you too much, when everything about you was amazing."

"I bet when you were little, you expected a girl to know that you liked her when you stopped beating her up. You can stare; I like it. You can give me compliments; I like them. I'm afraid I'm going to be the one who takes the lead and controls the pace of this relationship." She went to the door, threw the deadbolt and turned out the outside light.

"Are you ready to trust me?"

CHAPTER FORTY-SEVEN

Juan went to work, anxiously waiting to hear about how the attempt on Morrison's life worked out. He waited as long as he could before he called Collins.

"Hello, who is this?"

"Sorry to wake you, but I had to know how the plan worked."

"Oh yeah, I should have called you. The sniper did his job and got away without any problems. We're waiting for the target's reaction. He hasn't reported the incident yet. I'm not sure the plan is going to work. The man is a trained detective. He might have figured out something was up when he didn't turn up dead. Littlefield and I will have to play it cool in the office tomorrow and see what happens."

"If Morrison doesn't turn on Omar, that tells me that he's not afraid of him. If I were Morrison, I'd take out some insurance in case I died suddenly," said Juan.

"You're right, so would I."

"If our plan doesn't work, we should find out if Morrison has a lawyer, a will or a safety deposit box somewhere."

"Good idea. But our plan still might work. Let's not get ahead of ourselves."

"Please call me tomorrow."

"Okay, goodnight." Collins hung up the phone and fell back into bed. He thought about the acting job he and

Littlefield had to pull off in the morning. They had to pretend that they didn't know anything about the attempt on Morrison's life. Morrison would probably be watching them like a hawk to try and confirm his suspicions.

Collins was sick of this case. It had gone on too long with too little to show for the manpower expended. The brass wasn't going to put up with it for too much longer. He had to catch a break. He thought about the last thing that Juan had said. *"Maybe Morrison did take out insurance. And if he died, the case might break wide open. Enough wishful thinking, the near miss plan might still work."*

Sanders woke up in strange surroundings. He saw the pink curtains and white vanity table with eyes still half asleep. His mind caught up and he heard the soft breathing next to him. He turned over carefully and he saw her. Her hair was a mess and her makeup was smudged. She was still beautiful. He finally had a chance to stare at her and he did.

He started replaying last night's love scene in his mind. He remembered how she felt and how she smelled. She turned out the lights. He wished she hadn't. He wanted to watch her as they made love. He wanted to look into her eyes and to see the movements of her mouth. He didn't remember stopping. He didn't want to stop. He fell asleep so quickly; it was as though he passed out. How many times did they do it? Three or four, he didn't remember. He hoped he didn't hurt or frighten her.

She stirred and woke with a big smile. He relaxed. She didn't appear to be frightened and she kissed him. "How are you?" she asked.

"Happy, very happy."

"I'm glad I didn't disappoint."

"Please don't trivialize what happened last night. It was very important to me."

"It was important to me too, but let's not get too serious. There's plenty of time for that. We're supposed to be having fun. Relax."

"Fun, relax? Being with you is the most frightening thing I've ever experienced. I'm scared to death that I'll do something to make you mad and kick me out."

"I don't know what I'm going to do with you. I like you a lot. You've got to realize that I'm not going to kick you out without a good reason. After last night, it's going to have to be a very good reason. For all I know, you just might kick me to the curb."

"Never."

"We'll see. For now, this is how it is. I'm your girlfriend, your only girlfriend. And you're my one and only. If you need a date for an FBI Ball, I expect to be invited. If you need anything of a personal nature from a member of the opposite sex, I'm the one you call. And it works the same way for me. Can you live with that?"

"You bet I can." They both laughed and kissed.

Bonnie looked at the clock and said, "Good, it's still early. I have time to send you off to work with a smile.

CHAPTER FORTY EIGHT

Collins and Littlefield met in the parking lot and walked into work together. Morrison hadn't showed up yet. They agreed to treat Morrison the same way they did before they left for the weekend, with complete contempt. They got their coffee and went into the conference room to call Internal Affairs to get an update.

"John Smith, Internal Affairs."

"Good morning, John. This is Collins and Littlefield just checking in."

"Good morning, guys, I don't have anything new to tell you."

"Did you arrange for us to have a conference call with your FBI friend?"

"I put in a call to him. He hasn't called back yet."

"Tell us, John, are you anywhere near to charging Morrison for anything?"

"No, not yet; these things take time."

Collins resisted making a snide remark about the pace of IA investigations. "I know, John, but all good things have to come to an end." He couldn't resist after all.

"We're still gathering evidence."

"John, does the evidence you have so far add up to be enough for you to get a court order to open Morrison's safety deposit box, if he has one?"

"No, but if we have reason to believe that the contents of the box contains evidence of criminal wrongdoing, we can get it open."

"Great! We believe that Morrison took out some insurance to protect himself against Omar."

"Okay, where is the box and how do we know what's in the box?"

"We don't know where it is, but maybe you do. Did your guys tail him to any bank?"

"You saw the report on his movements. No bank. What about my second question, how do you know what's in the box?"

"We have a strong hunch."

"A hunch won't cut it, no matter how strong. We need evidence or firsthand knowledge of the box's contents."

"Shit." Collins couldn't hold back his frustration. "In other words, we can't get in the box."

"Not without a legitimate reason. You got anything else?"

"No that's it, talk to you soon." Collins turned off the speakerphone. "I think IA is holding out on us again. Everyone has a bank and they visit it regularly. I'm sure they know where the box is. But they're right about us not having a good enough reason to access it."

"Do you think we should put our own tail on him again?"

"There's an easier way. We'll call payroll and find out if his checks are direct deposited."

"Of course, I should have thought of that."

As they were leaving the conference room, Morrison walked in. They glared at each other. Morrison said. "Littlefield, you coward, the next time you want to take a shot at me, get close enough so I can return fire."

"You're so dirty you'd leave a ring around Lake Okeechobee." Littlefield countered.

"Be careful, or you might experience your own near miss," Morrison said, as he walked off back to the elevators.

"He figured it out," said Littlefield.

"Ya think? Our only chance now is to find out where he keeps his insurance policy and get ahold of it."

Payroll provided the name of Morrison's bank. Collins called the local branch and found out, after being passed around from bank officer to bank officer, that Morrison had a safety deposit box there. Collins was also able to find out that Morrison had accessed the box a week ago.

Collins spent the rest of the day talking to the Chief of Detectives and the Assistant District Attorney. All his talking got him nowhere. He didn't have enough to get a court order to have Morrison's box opened. He wasn't even close.

He was pissed. The system was obstructing him, IA was lying to him and Morrison was about to get away with murder.

Morrison left the station in a rage. He had planned to spend the day staring at Collins and Littlefield until they gave themselves away. But he couldn't do it. The moment he saw them, he knew that they had done it. During his outburst, there were no denials from them.

Morrison needed to do something to lift his spirits. He called Omar and arranged to have Anwar deliver the twenty thousand to him in the local branch of the East Midland Bank.

He killed a half an hour in the corner Starbucks and then went to the bank. He stopped at the counter and pretended to fill out a deposit slip. Anwar walked up to him, handed him a package and walked away. Morrison went to a teller and asked for access to his safety deposit box.

In the booth, Morrison opened the package and counted the money. He put the money in the safety deposit box and closed it. Counting the money helped his mood. Early retirement was just a little bit closer. He had the box put away and was leaving the bank when the Loan Officer stopped him.

"I hope everything worked out okay."

"Excuse me?"

"You're Mr. Morrison, aren't you?"

"Detective Morrison. What's this about?"

"We had a call earlier inquiring whether or not you had a safety deposit box here with us. I don't know why they transferred it to me. I'm a loan officer."

"Oh, yeah. That was just a little personnel matter. They needed to know where to locate all my assets in case of death in the line of duty."

"I'm glad it's all straightened out. Have a good day."

"You too." Morrison was stunned. They were closing in on him. They found out that he had a box. Now they knew where it was. If they could get to the box, it would be all over. His head started pounding. He had to calm down and think. He left the bank and instead of going to his car, he kept walking up the street.

Anwar was waiting outside the bank, not planning to

tail Morrison, just to observe. He spotted Morrison coming out of the bank without the package. He knew that twenty thousand was too much to have deposited; banks report deposits that large. He figured that Morrison must have a box in the bank. Anwar went to his car and drove off.

Morrison took a long walk. He tried to decide if the documents and money were safe in the box. He was sure that they had nothing on him and they couldn't justify a court order to have his box opened. He had to remain calm. Everything would go away. It was just a matter of time. He needed to walk some more before he went back to the office. Otherwise, he might take a shot at Littlefield and he would have no intention of missing.

Sanders went to work happy. He had never been so happy. He found it hard to believe that his world had changed so drastically since he left the office on Friday night. He sat at his desk for a half an hour trying to focus on his work. He couldn't. His thoughts kept drifting back to Bonnie. She was too good to be true; he knew it. She had to be using him. They'd have grandchildren before he'd believe that she had no ulterior motive. However, if she was deceiving him, she was putting her all into the deception effort. He decided to hold back and not get invested in this relationship.

He laughed. *"Fat chance,"* he thought to himself. The phone rang and he was glad for the interruption.

"Agent Sanders speaking."

"Ron, this is John Smith. I've been trying to reach you since last week."

"What's up?"

"Our boys, Collins and Littlefield, found out about your involvement in this case."

"How'd they do that?"

"I don't know. They just called and accused me of working with you behind their backs. They want a three way conversation."

"I can't tell them anything that will help their case."

"I know, but they see conspiracies everywhere. They want to know all the players and they want to be assured that nothing is being held back."

"When you talk to them again, you can tell them that I have nothing to contribute. Tell them that if they want me to be directly involved, I'll be happy to take over the case. FBI Agents don't operate in support roles, but our laboratories and technicians stand ready to help. That should put them off."

"I'm sure it will. But the boys are still plugging away. Their latest theory is that Morrison took out an insurance policy and put all he knows about Omar and his operation on paper and locked it in his bank safety deposit box."

"That sounds plausible." Sanders sat up straight and leaned forward attentively.

"Yes it does. They want me to get a court order to open Morrison's box."

"Good luck. It takes an act of God to open a box."

"I know. We don't have enough on him to get a court order. So another good idea bites the dust."

"Too bad."

"Yeah, things went south for us when Morrison bought that new phone. Wait a minute. Can your FBI technicians listen in on a cell phone call if they know when and where the phone is being used?"

"We can't, but I'm sure my friends over at NSA can."

"Can you set it up?"

"Yeah, sure; if the guy tailing Morrison lets us know when he's using the phone, we can get it recorded."

"Great. We should have thought of this before. Set it up. We'll nail this bastard yet."

Anwar met Omar in his office. There had been a number of recent improvements in the office. There was a new paint job. Eggshell-white wasn't too original, but it improved the place a lot. He had also added a new desk chair and a couple of landscape paintings. The office looked clean and impersonal, just the way Omar wanted.

"Did you give him the money?" Omar asked before Anwar sat down.

"Yes, he's got it."

"Did he say anything?"

"No, he just stepped away. I did see him again outside the bank."

"You didn't tail him, did you? I don't want any more shit with that guy."

"No, no I didn't tail him. I just saw him walk away without the package."

Robert C. Stewart

"He left it in the bank?"

"Yes, he must have a safety deposit box there. He couldn't have deposited it. There would have been questions to answer and extra forms to fill out."

"The box could be where his insurance policy is. This is interesting information. Now that we know that the policy is beyond our reach, we have to make it beyond everyone else's reach," said Omar.

"I don't understand. What are you saying?"

"I've been thinking about this for a while. It takes two things to insure Morrison's protection. The first thing is the policy itself; all the information that can be used against us. The second thing is someone to bring it to light; someone to turn it over to the proper authorities."

"A lawyer!"

"Yes. We have to find who Morrison's lawyer is and have a little talk with him."

"What good would that do?"

"Anwar, catch up. If the lawyer has instructions to open the box upon Morrison's death, we kill the lawyer, and destroy the instructions. Then after Morrison disappears, the box remains unopened until Morrison is found or declared dead. We will make absolutely sure that he is never found. I believe it takes seven years to declare someone dead, that's if someone wants to."

"What happens after seven years?"

"By then the information in the box will no longer be relevant. We can change our operations and move them elsewhere. Who knows? In seven years time, you'll probably be running things."

That sounded good to Anwar and he said, "I'll find the lawyer as soon as possible."

CHAPTER FORTY-NINE

Sanders realized that he had to throw himself into his work and stop thinking about Bonnie if he was going to get anything done. He was glad Smith had tasked him with working with the NSA to intercept Morrison's phone calls. Weeding his way through the interagency bureaucracy would take him most of the week. He pulled out a pad of paper in order to keep track of the liaison officers and interagency specialists he'd have to talk to in order to set up the intercept.

Four hours and thirteen calls later, he got a promise of a return call from someone who could help him. However, the call wouldn't come through until the next day. It was well past the lunch hour and he thought that if he went to the restaurant, she might have time for him. He headed out.

The drive to the restaurant wasn't bad. It was well after 1:00 pm and the traffic had died down. It was hot and humid and he had the air-conditioner going full blast. He noticed that he wasn't annoyed by as many things as he used to be. And he didn't give a second thought to the car taking up two spaces in the parking lot. However, he kicked its tires as he walked past.

He entered the restaurant and walked to the hostess station. "Is it too late for lunch?"

The hostess turned to him and flashed a look of recognition. "Not for you, sir," she said with a broad smile, as she showed him to a pretty good table. "Sorry about the noise. We're starting to set up for the evening meal. Shall I tell her you're here?"

"If she's busy don't disturb her."

"If I don't tell her, I'll get in trouble." She smiled again and walked away.

After a few minutes, Bonnie came to the table. "You're late for lunch," she said, as she sat down quickly, before Sanders could rise and hold her chair.

"I suspected I might be too late, but she seated me anyway. I got the feeling that I was getting special treatment."

Bonnie blushed. "I came into work a little too happy today. I gave myself away. We're like one big family here, I had to tell the girls about you."

"How much did you tell?"

"I just told them about our date, walking through the museum and the art galleries. They guessed the rest. I'll go see what they have left over from the lunch menu. I'll be back in a minute."

Sanders sat there fully aware of the looks and giggles directed at him from all corners of the restaurant. It was awkward and uncomfortable. It was high school all over again.

Bonnie came back with his lunch under a metal plate cover. She set the plate down and removed the cover to reveal grilled salmon, scalloped potatoes and French cut green beans. "It looks delicious," he said.

"It better be." She noticed the waitresses staring and giggling. She flashed a stern look in their direction and everyone returned to a business-like posture.

She watched him eat and made small talk. He enjoyed the meal and the company. "Will I see you tonight?" she asked.

"I don't know. Don't you want to catch your breath? Don't you want to have some time to yourself?"

"Do you?" she said, with a hurt look in her eyes.

"NO! Bonnie, I don't want to mess this up by pressuring you or not allowing you your space."

"Space is overrated."

"What time should I drop by?"

"Don't come if you don't want to."

"Bonnie, remember I'm crazy about you."

Bonnie became flushed and even more beautiful. "I'll be home around ten." She got up and went back to work.

CHAPTER FIFTY

Anwar instructed one of his men to watch Morrison from a distance. He was to be watched just to be sure of his whereabouts while his apartment was being searched. As it turned out, watching Morrison wasn't necessary, he only went to his apartment to eat and sleep, the rest of the time he was either at work or his neighborhood bar.

The apartment break-in went smoothly. The neighbors minded their own business and none of them liked Morrison anyway. The lady next door made the mistake of asking Morrison for a cup of milk once, the resulting tirade of expletives left her in shock.

The apartment was searched from top to bottom; however, there were no papers, business cards or refrigerator magnets associated with any lawyer or law firm. Anwar's man planted a sound activated bug near the telephone answering machine. The apartment was a mess before the break in and Anwar's man left it just as he found it.

Then Anwar made a list of every law firm within a half-mile radius of the 4th Street Police Station. The thinking was that Morrison was too lazy to go too far to find a lawyer. There were eighteen names on the list. Anwar broke the list into the names of individual lawyers in the firms and the list grew to seventy-eight names. Eliminating the Environmental, Patent, Tax and Corporate lawyers and other non-related areas, the list came down to twenty-six. Anwar got what he wanted, a list of the names and numbers of the lawyers likely to be working for Morrison.

Later that afternoon, Anwar had Kamil, one of his men, meet him at his apartment. This was an honor for Kamil; he had never been invited to Anwar's home before.

"My friend," said Anwar, "I have a special task for you."

Kamil was a bit apprehensive. He and Anwar had always been on good terms. But Anwar had never shown him any favors or attention. Kamil wondered why he was chosen for a special task.

"Have I done something wrong, Anwar?"

"No, no, this is not a punishment or anything like that."

Kamil was relieved. He had tried hard to win Anwar's favor and he was loyal beyond question.

"Relax, Kamil. I just want you to make a few phone calls." Anwar gave him the list of lawyers' names and numbers. Kamil's qualification for the task was that he had no accent. Anwar had prepared the script.

"When you call these people, this is what I want you to say." Anwar handed Kamil the script.

"When do you want me to call them?"

"Call them tonight. You will be talking to their answering machines, so I want you to get it right the first time. No mistakes."

Kamil practiced the script over and over until he was sure that he was ready. He had no intention of disappointing Anwar. The script read:

Hello <u>*lawyer's name*</u> *this is Ken Morrison. Sorry to call you so late, but it's urgent that I speak to you as soon as possible. Call me at home when you get this.*

That night, Kamil called each of the twenty-six names on the list. He did his job perfectly.

CHAPTER FIFTY-ONE

Collins and Littlefield had run out of ideas. After talking to the Assistant District Attorney, Collins suspected that Internal Affairs would never have enough of a case to get a court order to open Morrison's box. "I don't know what else to do. We've tried everything, even breaking the law." Collins was at the point of giving up.

"I know, but the thought of Morrison and his murdering buddies getting away clean is killing me," said Littlefield.

"I was going to wait until tonight to call the kid, but I think I'll go ahead and call him now."

Collins hit the speaker and dialed the number. It rang twice. "Hello."

"Good afternoon, kid. I hope I woke you, I still owe you for your last call to me."

"No, you didn't wake me," he lied. "I'm awake. How did it go?"

"No luck. He saw right through it. He even blamed Littlefield directly for the shooting."

"Well, I guess he's not as dumb as we thought he was," said Juan. "What's next?"

"That's it, kid. We've run out of ideas. It looks like we'll have to put this case in the unsolved pile."

"Morrison won't lead us to Omar. Hey, can't we find him on our own? How many Omars are there in the city? Do you guys have access to a telephone listing in order of first name?"

"One question at a time. We could probably find a few Omars that fit the bill and then narrow the list down. But what do we have even if we find him? We've gotten nothing on him unless Morrison implicates him in the murders or some other crime."

"If you find him, you'll find the crime. I'm only a teenager, but it seems to me that we've already broken the law. So why not do what the old-time cops did? Catch the bad guy and worry about the crime later. I'm sure he picked his feet in Poughkeepsie."

Collins and Littlefield laughed out loud. It took several minutes for them to compose themselves. "You've been watching too many old movies, kid. But it's an idea and Littlefield and I are all out. So, I guess we've got a new plan."

"Do you guys think you can find him with just his first name?"

"We can give it a shot. If he's got a driver's license, land line, or a place of residence, we've got a good chance of finding him."

"Well good luck guys, I'm going back to sleep."

"I thought you said you were awake?"

"Yeah, right. Bye."

"That kid's a piece of work," said Collins, still chuckling.

Sanders showed up at Bonnie's door at 10:00 pm on the

dot. Before he could ring the bell, the door opened. "I knew you'd be there, right on time."

"I'm going to surprise you and be late one of these days."

"You don't have to change your ways for me. I like you just the way you are." She kissed him and took his hand, leading him into the living room. "I hope you've eaten because I've already cleaned up the kitchen."

"Yes, I've eaten."

"Good. I just want to curl up next to you and watch some TV until bed-time."

"So you've got the evening all planned, have you?"

"That's right. I spend most of my day thinking about you anyway, so I might as well make plans for the time we spend together."

He took her in his arms and held her tight. "You have no idea how happy I am," he said.

"I think I do." She walked him to the sofa and they sat. "How was your day?" she said, as she reached for the remote.

"There's nothing new on your case."

"That's not what I meant."

"Come on, someone tried to kill you, you've got to be concerned about the progress on the case."

"I suppose I am, but it's not the only thing I'm concerned about. Your job is dangerous and I want to know about it. The truth is, I'm more worried about you than I am about me. I think whoever tried to kill me made a mistake. I'm not a threat to anyone. If they wanted to prevent me from talking to the police, they missed their chance. I've already talked to the police. I think I'm safe."

"You're probably right. I should have told you that myself."

"Yes, you should have. But you were afraid that I wouldn't need you anymore, weren't you?"

"Maybe a little."

"Okay, we both know that I don't need you to keep me safe. Now all you have to worry about is keeping me happy." He kissed her tenderly and she smiled. "That's a good start."

CHAPTER FIFTY-TWO

Littlefield was the first to get the news; the team working on the double homicide was being disbanded. The bosses couldn't justify the expenditures and other cases were piling up. He knew it had to happen. The word was that he and Collins had two weeks to wrap up the case. It was expected that most of their time was to be spent making sure all the paper work was completed.

The detectives started chasing down the name 'Omar'. The NCIC database was accessed for any reference to the name. DMV files were queried as well as phone directories sorted by first name. They hoped that Omar was the man's real name and not some nickname or alias. They came up with seventy-one possibilities.

"Wait a minute. I think that IA and the FBI guy already know who Omar is. Or at least they know how to find him," said Collins.

"If they know how to find him, why haven't they done it already?"

"Because they were thinking like we were. They wanted something on him first."

"What do they have that we don't?"

"They had a tap on Morrison's phones. That means back when the tap was working, they got the number Morrison called. They got Omar's number. With that number, we can get Omar's full name from the phone company."

Collins and Littlefield went to the conference room to call Internal Affairs. This was one phone call neither one of them wanted to make. "Are you sure we want to make this call? This guy lied to us I don't know how many times."

"Yeah, we gotta make the call. Even his lies may tell us something." Collins turned on the speakerphone and dialed the number.

"John Smith, Internal Affairs."

"Good morning, John. This is Collins and Littlefield again. We haven't been lied to yet this morning, so we thought we'd give you a call. How are you?"

"Come on guys, be nice."

"John, we need one thing from you. We need the number Morrison called to get Omar, back when the phone tap was working."

"What good is that going to do you?"

"I don't know why we have to tell you everything and you tell us nothing."

"Okay, I got the number here. Give me a minute." A minute later, Smith said, "The number is 105-6327."

"Thanks. In answer to your question, this number combined with a phone company warrant should get me Omar's full name."

"What good is that when you've got nothing on him?"

"First we'll find him, and then we'll find something on him."

"John, if this number is bogus, I'm going to come up there and give you a reason to bring charges against me."

"That's the number we got from our tap. By the way, I

talked to Agent Sanders. He said he had nothing to add to your investigation, but the FBI lab and technicians stand ready to help."

"That's pretty much what I expected," said Collins. "That's all we need; thanks for the number."

"Glad I could help."

Collins turned off the speakerphone. "Let's see where this number takes us."

John Smith knew the case against Morrison was going nowhere. The tail on him had been a waste of time for the last two weeks. He hoped that Sanders was able to arrange the call intercept with the NSA. He called Agent Sanders to find out where things stood.

"Hello, this is Agent Sanders."

"Hi, Ron, this is John Smith. I'm wondering how things went with the NSA and if they caught any calls yet."

"It wasn't easy, but I got things set up. Unfortunately, Morrison hasn't made a call to Omar yet. They're probably not on the best of terms right now. If he does call, I bet it will be something important."

"I think you're right. If you don't mind me saying so, you seemed to have lost interest in Omar and the other guy, Azlan."

"Azlan is more than likely landfill by now. And as for Omar, we've got nothing on him, so what's the point of going after him. We would have to set up surveillance and spend money watching him and hope we'd catch him doing something. It would be a waste of the bureau's time," said Sanders.

"That's the opposite position our detective friends are taking. They're going old school. They're going to find him and then try to pin something on him."

"How are they going to find him?"

"I gave them the number Morrison used to call him back when our phone tap was working. With the number and a warrant, they expect to get his full name from the telephone company."

"Of course, good thinking... I mean, the FBI would never condone such a course of action. They'd be breaking the law, trumping up charges against Omar. That's outrageous. However, if they have any trouble getting the warrant, I have the names of a few friendly judges I can give them."

"If they have any trouble, I'll let them know. Thanks for setting up the NSA intercept. Let's hope it turns up something we can use. Talk to you soon." Smith hung up.

CHAPTER FIFTY-THREE

Ben Springer went to work in a foul mood. The newborn had cried all night and the wife somehow convinced him to alternate baby care shifts with her. He was up every four hours, but he woke up at every shift. He loved them both, but he couldn't take much more of this. "Damn-it," he thought, "I work all day long, I'm a lawyer; I can negotiate a better deal than this."

He entered the Law Offices of Haden and Winston. He resented the smiling face of his secretary and returned her smile with a smirk. Irene wasn't offended; she knew what he was going through at home. She took it in stride, just like all the other little indignities she had to put up with. "Good morning, Mr. Springer. There's an urgent message on your machine. You can play it back by hitting '*98' on your phone."

"Thank you, Irene." He hated to be attacked with work before he got settled and had a cup of coffee. But that was one of Irene's ways of getting back at him for his many offenses.

Ben put down his briefcase and sat at his desk. He fired up his computer, put in his password and looked at his calendar. His day didn't look too bad. He just had a couple of meetings and a deposition to prepare for. He picked up the phone and dialed *98. He listened to the message twice. Morrison's message disturbed him for two reasons: first its mysterious undertone and second, it didn't sound like Morrison. Ben looked up Morrison's home number and dialed it. The answering machine picked up and he left a message.

The bug that Anwar's man had put in Morrison's apartment relayed the message Ben Springer left on the answering machine.

"Ken, this is Ben Springer from Haden and Winston returning your call. I'll be in the office all morning. Get back to me when you can. I hope you get over your cold soon. You sound terrible."

Anwar listened to the recording and laughed. "We have the lawyer. Soon, we'll put an end to Detective Ken Morrison." He was very pleased with himself and he knew Omar would be pleased as well. Anwar was tempted to call Omar, but he changed his mind. He would deliver this news in person.

Anwar drove to Omar's auto repair shop. He entered the office and his demeanor told Omar that he had good news. "I found the lawyer!" Anwar explained in detail how he had bugged Morrison's apartment and used the answering machine to find the lawyer.

"I knew you would not fail me." Omar stood and embraced Anwar. "Excellent. Now we must proceed with caution. We have to get the lawyer to give us Morrison's instructions. Then we can get rid of him and Morrison is ours."

"What do we do next?"

"We have to observe the lawyer and find out his routine. We have to get him in his office alone. We also need to know about the security in the lawyer's building. It would be good if he works late after everyone else has gone. Then we can force him to give us the instructions, and then take him for a ride, as they used to say. If we can't get him alone at the office, then we'll grab him outside and take him there when the place is empty."

"Do we have a time constraint?"

"The sooner, the better. But take a couple of days and watch the lawyer's movements. Find out if he's married and if he has friends. It would be best if he had an accident after he gives us Morrison's instructions. Start thinking about how his accident is going to happen. While you're at it, give some thought to how Detective Morrison is going to die. My only requirement for him is that it not be quick."

CHAPTER FIFTY-FOUR

Morrison got the good news that the double homicide team was no more. Only Collins and Littlefield were left and they had cleanup duty. Morrison was elated; the nightmare was coming to an end. He was still pissed that Littlefield had taken a shot at him. If he could find a way to get payback, he would.

Morrison thought it would be a good idea to call Omar and tell him that the investigation was almost over. He decided to make the call after lunch. He could feel the weight of the world slowly being lifted from his shoulders.

He looked over at Ann thumbing through case files. She looked good. "How are you doing today?"

"Not bad." Ann was surprised at the question. "Where's that coming from? Usually, you've got nothing to say to me in the morning."

"Just trying to be nice. You look good today. I like your outfit."

"Are you dying or something?"

"Can't a guy spread a little joy around? There was a time when you responded to my charm."

"That was a long time ago and it was a bad idea back then. You can turn off the charm, it's wasted on me."

"Okay, I'll go back to my regular self. I just remembered the old days and I had to test the waters again." He was in such a good mood; he even enjoyed being rejected by Ann.

After lunch, Morrison called Omar. The phone rang three times.

"Hello."

"Hello, Omar, for a minute there I thought you weren't accepting my calls," said Morrison.

"Our last call wasn't too friendly and it cost me."

"I got good news. They're disbanding the team that was working the case. The investigation is going on the shelf."

"That is good news. I guess our association will also come to an end."

"No. No reason for that. I'm sure I can still be of service to you."

"That may be true, but you were so upset with your involvement in this case that I assumed that once it was over, you'd disassociate yourself from me and my operation."

"It did get tense for a while, but things can be overlooked. I think we can continue to work together, especially since the paydays are bigger."

"That last payment was a onetime fee."

"No, that was one installment of a periodic fee," said Morrison.

"We'll have to talk about that."

"That's what we're doing, my friend. That's what we're doing."

"I'll have to think this over. I'll be on vacation for a few days, but I'll get back to you. I like to get away every once in awhile. It helps to recharge my batteries. You should try it. I know you can afford it now." Omar laughed a forced laugh.

"That's not a bad idea. Now that the pressure's off, I should get away for a couple of days."

"Have you got anything else to tell me?"

"No, that's it."

"Take care of yourself." Omar hung up.

CHAPTER FIFTY-FIVE

"Omar Haider, that's the name on the account." Collins had just finished talking to the phone company representative. "We've finally got something to work with."

"I'll check the phone book for the name 'Haider'. I don't think there'll be too many. We can also look into the Property Tax Database; if he owns a house, he paid taxes on it. If he has a job or owns a business, we'll find out. By the end of the day we'll know what this guy eats for breakfast." Littlefield hadn't been this excited since he took a shot at Morrison.

"This isn't going to be easy now that we're all by ourselves," said Collins. "Once we locate this guy, we're going to have to tail him and find his associates. It's a lot for two guys to do while they're cleaning up the paperwork to close down an investigation."

"Maybe some of our ex-teammates will work for us off the books?"

"I'll ask around, but first, let's find out everything we can about Omar."

From his desk, Morrison could see the sudden energy and enthusiasm Collins and Littlefield were putting into their work. He didn't think that they caught a new case this quickly. He watched them carefully. They were being close-mouthed about what they were doing. He asked, but nobody knew anything. They couldn't keep anything quiet for very long. He just had to wait. He was eventually going to find out what was up.

Anwar's biggest flaw was his lack of patience. He didn't want to wait and watch the lawyer. He wanted to act now, and get to Morrison as soon as he could. But this time, Anwar was going to do what he was told. He followed the lawyer from his house, in the morning, to work and back again.

He had people following the wife. The wife took the newborn to the market in the morning. They took a walk around the block in the afternoon. She greeted her husband at the door when he came home after work. She more than greeted him, she attacked him, wanting to hear something more than TV or baby sounds.

So far, Anwar found out that within minutes of the time the lawyer was taken, he would be missed. He also found that someone was in the law offices for at least two hours after Springer had left for the day. The plan that Anwar had come up with was: to take Springer after work, have him phone his wife and tell her that he had to work late, sit on him until the building cleared, force him to give up Morrison's instructions and then stage a traffic accident, a fatal one.

Anwar couldn't find any flaws in the plan. He called Omar and told him that a second day of tailing the lawyer wasn't necessary. He explained the plan and told him that he would carry it out the next day. Omar agreed.

Juan went through his normal routine at work, cleaning the restrooms and emptying the trash in the offices. He wasn't anxious to get to the conference room. He knew the case was being closed down and that meant that all the information would be taken down off the walls and the boards and packed away.

It seemed to him like somebody else had died. After all, the case was a living thing to him. It had been dying for a while and now it was going to be buried in the property room and the case files. It was very sad. Juan didn't talk to the detectives every night and he hoped that this was one of those nights when they didn't call. No such luck.

His phone rang. "Hello, this is Juan."

"How are you doing, kid?"

"Not so good. Not closing a case the right way sucks."

"I hear that. We found Omar's full name. It's Omar Haider. We're in the process of finding out everything we can about him. We'll do what we can to dig up some dirt on this guy. If he's stupid and isn't hiding his illegal activities, we'll nail him. More than likely, we'll have to sit on him for a long time before we get something on him."

"Well I guess it's better than nothing."

"Just barely. It will take a week or so before we can wrap everything up and catch a new case, so take it easy for a few days. Don't let this case get you down. We can't win them all."

"I sure hate losing them."

"Me too, kid. We'll get them next time."

CHAPTER FIFTY-SIX

It was 1:00 am when Morrison made it home. He usually closed the bar, but tonight, he didn't feel like drinking himself shitfaced. He walked into the apartment and performed his little ritual of putting his badge and gun on a shelf in the bookcase. He hung his jacket on the back of a kitchen chair, and the light on the phone answering machine caught his eye. He remembered he saw it flashing the night before, but he was too drunk to care. He didn't pay any attention to it this morning either; the flashing light was hard to see in the daylight.

The only time he got messages was during political campaigns or telemarketing assaults. He pressed the play button.

"Ken, this is Ben Springer from Haden and Winston returning your call. I'll be in the office all morning. Get back to me when you can. I hope you get over your cold soon. You sound terrible."

Morrison stopped breathing. He was motionless for a minute. He wasn't a great detective, but he was a man who had earned his way into the position. He picked up his cell phone.

"Hello, who is this? Do you know what time it is?"

"Omar, this is Morrison. I see you found one of my lawyers."

There was no sound on the other end of the call. "What are you talking about?"

"Cut the crap, Omar. You obviously don't respect me. The case is almost over and you're still trying to get to me."

"I don't know what you're talking about. You're talking crazy. Why did you call me at this hour?"

"Shut up, Omar. Listen. I have one safety deposit box, but I have more than one lawyer with instructions to open it upon my death. Killing one lawyer will do you no good. I'm disappointed in you, my friend. Your operations are about to have major disruptions. The DEA will be waiting for your people at the next drug delivery. And ATF is dying to get a lead related to that shoot-out they had recently."

"Okay, Morrison, stop. Don't do anything foolish. If I go down, you'll go down."

"I don't intend to take you down. I'm just going to fuck with you like you're fucking with me. Your business is going to take a little hit, that's all. I figure you'll lose about a hundred grand in merchandise and a third of your people before the anonymous tips stop going to the federal agencies."

"Don't do this!"

"Why not? You fuck with me, and I fuck with you. Isn't that how the game's played?"

"What can I do to make this right?"

"You can stop trying to kill me."

"Sorry, no more hostilities. I swear it."

"I don't trust you, Omar. That shouldn't surprise you. Tell you what. It's time for the second installment of my periodic fee. I'll meet Anwar at my bank tomorrow at noon."

"He'll be there."

Morrison signed off. He made a mental note to write a duplicate set of instructions and find an additional lawyer first thing tomorrow.

Omar didn't want to wait until morning to call Anwar. But he waited a few moments to compose himself. He dialed the number.

"Hello, who is this?"

"Anwar, you idiot. Morrison found out that we were trying to find his lawyer. You didn't erase his answering machine did you?"

Anwar was still trying to clear his head after waking from a deep sleep. "I ah... no, I didn't erase the message."

"Morrison got the message and put two and two together. He says that getting rid of the lawyer will do us no good, because he has more than one lawyer with instructions to open the box if something should happen to him."

"Do you believe him?"

"It doesn't matter. We can't take that chance. Leave the lawyer alone. You have another job to do."

"What must I do?"

"You are to pay Morrison another twenty thousand tomorrow at noon at his bank. And since you fucked up, ten thousand of it will be your money."

"My money?"

"You heard me. Failure has consequences. Morrison has bested us, and we will share the punishment. Deliver the money to him and call me when it's done. Remember, call me, I don't want to see you for a while." Omar hung up.

CHAPTER FIFTY-SEVEN

The next morning, Agent Sanders went to work less happy, but more focused. The previous night was the first night he had slept alone in four days. He hadn't called Bonnie or gone to the restaurant the day before, so she had no opportunity to invite him over to spend the night. He finally had a chance to catch his breath and think objectively about their relationship. He knew he was going to hear about it the next time he saw her, but he had to slow things down, even at the risk of screwing things up.

There was a phone message from his contact at the NSA that they intercepted two calls between Morrison and Omar. Sanders called his contact and got him to email transcripts of the two calls. One half hour later, the email was delivered. Sanders read the transcripts and forwarded them to John Smith. He made the call.

"John Smith, Internal Affairs."

"John, Ron Sanders. I got a couple of intercepted phone calls from my NSA friends. I just forwarded them to you. They should be in your mail box in a couple of minutes."

"It's something juicy, I hope."

"I'll leave it up to you to determine how important they are. In the first one, Morrison is gloating about the double murder case being closed out without resolution. In the second one, he's accusing Omar of trying to kill him and his lawyer. You'll find it interesting. He and Omar are not a happy couple."

"I can't wait to read the transcripts myself."

"Another thing you'll read. Morrison is going to get a payoff at noon today at his bank. If you catch him in the act, you'll have something to question him about, but nothing to charge him with. He can say he's accepting a loan from his good friend, Anwar."

"We'll see what we can do. Thanks for the help. Talk to you soon."

Smith got the email ten minutes later. He read the transcripts. He found the dialogue between Omar and Morrison very interesting. Things had changed since the last conversation that Smith monitored. Now Morrison had the upper hand. Smith thought about showing up for the payoff in Morrison's bank, but he realized that he had nothing. If he interrupted the payoff, he would tip his hand and Morrison would know that he was being tailed and his phone was still being tapped.

Collins and Littlefield had put together a detailed description of Omar Haider. Haider was 42 years of age and a naturalized citizen. According to the information gathered, he came to this country 14 years ago from Argentina. He was a lawyer and had military experience. He worked here as a mechanic and became a part owner in an auto body shop. He had no police record. He owned a house on Douglas Road, appraised at $346K. He was married with two sons, 12 and 10. He had checking and savings accounts at National Bank totaling $29K. That was his public face.

No one from the disbanded team volunteered to watch

Haider on their own time. Most of them were glad to get off a dead end case and move on to something new. The big push was to be associated with cleared cases. The guy with the most cleared cases on his record got ahead. It was as simple as that.

Without help, it was over, and Collins and Littlefield knew it. They continued to put together the paperwork to close out the case.

Bonnie was visibly upset when she went to work, and everyone could see it. She went directly to her office instead of her usual practice of catching up on the gossip with the waitresses. Everyone gave her time to get herself together, but they didn't hold out for long. After an hour, a delegation went to her office to confront her.

"You always say that we're a family," said Amy, the head waitress. "It's family time. What's wrong?"

"I don't want to talk about it." Bonnie gave them her stern look, which usually put them in their place.

"Yes, you do. Do you want us to work today? Nothing gets done until we know that you're all right."

Bonnie was ready to assert herself and take control, when it seemed like all the air went out of her. "Okay, he didn't call and he didn't come by. I haven't heard from him for almost two days. He leaves my bed in the morning and goes off to work and then nothing. He's always talking about wanting to give me space. He thinks I'm using him. To be honest, it started out that way. But it's not true now. I think this guy is the one. But I don't know if he really wants to be in this relationship."

"Calm down. Has he said anything that makes you think he wants out?"

"No. I guess not."

"Does he act like he cares about you? Does he compliment you?"

"Yes, he says the right thing and I believe he cares."

"What do you know about him? What's his favorite food? What's his favorite football team?"

"I don't know every little thing about him; we've only been together for a few days." Bonnie was embarrassed that she couldn't answer any of those questions about Ron.

"I think you put your finger on the problem. You're 'newly mates'. You need to back off and give the relationship time to grow. Let him take control. We saw the way he was looking at you the other day in the restaurant. Just give him a little time to realize and appreciate what he's got. And when he does call, don't chew his head off. Pretend that you've almost forgotten about him because you've been busy doing other things. Just be cool."

Bonnie saw the heads nodding in agreement with what was being said, and she saw the wisdom of it. "All right, I'll take it easy and let him take control. If he doesn't, then so be it.

Thank you for your advice, ladies. Now get back to work."

They all filed out of Bonnie's office, satisfied that they had saved the day.

CHAPTER FIFTY-EIGHT

Morrison had a busy morning. He met with an estate-planning lawyer and gave him instructions to be carried out in the event of his death. He was driving north on 95, heading back to the city. It was a clear, sunny day. It was hot and getting hotter. The interstate was always under construction, but it never seemed to hinder the traffic too much. He was still pissed at Omar for trying to get to him, but he knew that if the situation were reversed, he'd try to do the same thing.

He decided not to go into the office today. It had been a long time since he had a day off. It wasn't that he was a dedicated hard worker; he just had nothing better to do. Today he decided to spend the day at the dog track, after his transaction with Anwar at the bank. He'd take some of the twenty thousand and invest it in a greyhound or two and then try his hand at the card tables. It was going to be a good day.

Anwar's morning was also busy. He didn't have the resources that Omar had. He had to collect a few outstanding debts and deplete his savings to come up with the ten thousand that he needed to pay Morrison. He was furious that he had to give Morrison his own money. He swore that Morrison wouldn't die peacefully at a ripe old age.

Anwar lived beyond his means. He didn't live lavishly, but whatever he earned he spent or he loaned to his friends. Until recently, he expected to move up in the organization and earn more.

Collecting debts wasn't always easy, so Anwar armed himself just to emphasize the fact that he was serious.

Anwar's mood was hostile and he didn't want any excuses, he wanted his money. He knew that if he had been given sufficient time to get the money, he wouldn't need to use the threat of force, but he had no time to spare.

His first stop was at a barbershop downtown. It was 9:30 in the morning and he didn't want to waste any time. The owner of the barbershop, Abdul Adl, was a long time acquaintance of Anwar's. Abdul Adl owed Anwar six thousand dollars.

The shop appeared to be doing well. There were three active barber chairs and enough seating to accommodate twenty customers. Abdul Adl was working when Anwar walked in and he asked Abdul Adl to talk to him in the back room. Abdul Adl, sensing that the conversation wasn't going to be a pleasant one, motioned to Anwar that he would join him after he finished with his customer. Anwar went to the room and waited. Anwar wasn't happy about waiting, but he didn't want to start any trouble if he didn't have to.

Anwar waited for ten minutes. He paced back and forth while looking at his watch. He looked back into the shop and saw a different customer in Abdul Adl's chair. Anwar calmly walked into the shop and smashed Abdul Adl across the forehead with the barrel of his gun. The barber when down like he was shot.

Everyone in the shop started to stir and Anwar said, "Stop! Stay where you are." Anwar had a reputation as a man to be respected. That and the gun in his hand convinced everyone to do what they were told. "This business is between me and Abdul Adl. Don't involve yourselves."

Anwar got the barber to his feet and took him in the back room. Anwar left five minutes later with six thousand dollars. He was grateful that many of his countrymen didn't believe in banks. He hoped his next stop would be easier.

His next stop was only three blocks away. He pulled up to the house and turned off the engine. He was angry that he had to use force and embarrass Abdul Adl at his place of business. Their relationship would never be the same and he deeply regretted his actions. He got out of the car and walked to the door. He rang the bell and the door opened immediately. Gohar stood in the doorway with forty-five hundred dollars in his hands. He had obviously heard about the incident at the barbershop. He gave the money to Anwar. Gohar closed the door without saying a word.

The morning violence calmed Anwar for the moment and he headed for the bank. The street traffic was heavy, but he made it to the bank with two minutes to spare. He didn't want to be late; he wanted to do exactly what Omar told him to do. He parked the car in the bank lot. He walked up the stairs and entered the bank. He spotted Morrison and walked toward him. Anwar couldn't disguise the expression of hate on his face. His expression and his body language drew the attention of a security guard. The guard watched him cross the bank floor and head toward a man standing by himself at a counter.

Anwar walked across the bank floor with his jacket open. The guard saw the gun in Anwar's waistband. "Gun!" yelled the guard, and he immediately drew his weapon.

Anwar instinctively took out his gun and fired as he saw the guard level his weapon at him. The guard fired wildly as he was hit and fell to the floor.

Another guard from the other side of the bank floor came running with his gun drawn. He fired three shots at Anwar who had moved to his left to take cover behind a counter. Anwar returned fire and hit the second guard.

Anwar then turned and ran for the exit. The first guard saw Anwar break cover and fired five shots at him, hitting him twice. Anwar was badly wounded. The gunfire stopped, but the screaming in the bank continued for five minutes.

When the police arrived six minutes later, they found two dead and two wounded. One of the dead was a city police detective, Ken Morrison. One of the guards was shot to death, the other was slightly wounded. The bank robber, identified as Anwar Iwahib, was critically wounded.

Two hours later, Channel Six News reported the incident. Omar listened to the report in his office. He phoned his wife at home. He said four words to her and hung up. Omar cleaned out the safe in the office, putting the cash and the papers in an attaché case. He went to the parking lot and got in an SUV, not his own, and drove away. His wife sent text messages to her sons, emptied the wall safe, and got two packed suitcases from her bedroom and put them near the front door. Ten minutes later, Omar arrived and put the suitcases in the SUV, and he and his wife drove away. They drove to a Quick-Stop convenience store, two blocks from the school complex. Omar's sons were waiting for them in the parking lot. They got in the car and the family drove off.

Collins and Littlefield forgot themselves and stood cheering when they heard the news of Morrison's death. They looked around the squad room, hoping no one else saw them celebrating the death of a fellow officer. Embarrassed, they sat back down. Now they had to wait until Morrison's representative came forward and got the box opened. It was really going to happen. The people responsible for the double homicide were going to be brought to justice.

CHAPTER FIFTY-NINE

Sanders called Bonnie and told her that there was a break in the missing persons case, and that it was just a matter of time before they found out what happened to Azlan. She seemed disinterested. "How are you? I haven't heard from you for a couple of days."

"I'm fine. I've been busy with work. And I needed some time away from you to clear my head."

Bonnie didn't respond. She held her breath. This sounded like a kiss-off.

"Bonnie, did you hear me?"

"Yes, I heard you," she answered.

"I expected you to be more upset. Anyway, I needed some time to myself to figure things out. If I let things continue the way they have been, it would not turn out well. I'm a take-charge guy, and I wouldn't be able to let you run the relationship for very long. If we are going to be together, I have to be in control. At the very least, I have to be a full partner. We're going to have to slow things down. I really care about you and I hope you'll go along with me on this. What do you say?"

Bonnie started breathing again. "Okay, we'll try it your way."

"Great, are you free on Sunday? I'd like to cook dinner for you."

"Yes, I'm free. Should I bring anything?" she asked.

"You could bring a toothbrush."

She smiled and said, "I think I'm going to be okay with the slow method."

A week later, two lawyers came forward and petitioned the court to have Morrison's box opened. The contents were examined and turned over to the police department. The box contained four handwritten pages and a picture of Omar Haider taken from a cell phone. The pages described Omar's operation of drug trafficking and illegal weapons sales. Apparently, Morrison didn't know how many people worked for Omar. Morrison only named Anwar Iwahib and Hassan Jawwali. The pages also named Anwar and Hassan as the murderers of Joey Adams and Eddie Donovan.

Morrison explained how he was brought in to find Adams and Donovan after they had killed Azlan Yardim. He said that Adams and Donovan had to be found to retrieve some papers that they had stolen in the liquor store robbery.

Since the bank incident, Anwar had come out of intensive care and was expected to live. An examination of his gun revealed that it was the same gun that had killed Joey Adams. There was a nationwide manhunt for both Omar and Hassan. Hassan would be found four weeks later, living in a motel in Las Vegas. He was killed in a shoot-out with the local authorities. Omar Haider and his family disappeared.

The case of the double homicide was finally closed the

right way. The party that Collins and Littlefield held in the conference room lasted all day. They made a monumental mess. They saved some cake from the party for Juan. That night, both detectives were on hand to greet Juan when he showed up for work.

"Well, we did it, kid. The case is wrapped up."

"Congratulations, detectives. There's another one in your win column. It won't be long now before you two get bumped up in pay grade, and you deserve it."

"We all deserve congratulations, Juan."

"Do we all deserve a pay bump?"

"Well yeah, but as we discussed, we have limited funds for our CIs."

"I'm not worried about money," said Juan.

Collins looked relieved. "What do you want, kid?"

"I want to share responsibilities."

"What, I don't understand."

Juan went to the utility closet and he came back with two brooms. As he handed a broom to each detective, he said, "After every case closing celebration, I want you guys to join me in the cleanup. That'll be my bonus."

The detectives laughed and agreed. They both started cleaning up the mess.

Juan turned to them and said, "Oh, one more thing. Would one of you guys teach me how to shoot?"

###

CPSIA information can be obtained at www.ICGtesting.com
Printed in the USA
BVOW11s0844081215

429662BV00018B/97/P

9 780983 946106